THE VILLA FAUSTINO

Joanna loved her home in the Canary Islands, and she valued her old friendship with Ramón, the handsome and imperious Marqués de Orleron y Faustino—but she still hoped to revisit London, her birthplace. But was it the right time to go, now that the lovely blonde Candida was making no secret of her intention to marry Ramón?

Books you will enjoy
by KATRINA BRITT

IF TODAY BE SWEET

When Lori went to stay with her brother in Venice, he warned her about the romantic atmosphere of the place blinding her to the real thing. Yet in no time she found herself falling in love with the handsome Prince Mario Volleano—who was just the kind of man her brother had warned her about. . .

THE EMERALD GARDEN

For years a bitter family quarrel had kept Vinney apart from her mother and her sister Denise. Now, though, they were all together again, and Vinney was hoping for a happier relationship at last. But all she succeeded in doing was to fall in love with the man her sister was going to marry . . .

GIRL IN BLUE

The beautiful Nora Staffordly had already caused Felicity heartbreak enough when she helped to wreck her beloved brother's life—but at least the episode had led to Felicity meeting a man she came to love even more than she had loved her brother: Curt Moreau. And then Nora came along to take that love from her too.

THE SPANISH GRANDEE

The imposing Spaniard Don Ramón de Biver y Aldenez had once been an important and romantic figure in Venetia's young life. Now, years later, they had met again, this time in his own country. Now he seemed to have no time for her at all—and why should he, when all his thoughts were for his tragic young fiancée?

THE VILLA FAUSTINO

BY

KATRINA BRITT

MILLS & BOON LIMITED
17–19 FOLEY STREET
LONDON W1A 1DR

First published 1977
This edition 1977

ISBN 0 263 72375 5

Made and printed in Great Britain by
Richard Clay (The Chaucer Press), Ltd., Bungay, Suffolk

CHAPTER ONE

It was one of those mornings when one felt that life could not be sweeter. The terrace, smothered in scarlet oleander and plumbago, drowsed dreamily in the warm golden sun above green lawns shaded by heavy branches of deep pink and cream bougainvillaea. In the Indian laurel, the birds were bursting forth in vociferous chirping and everywhere was the quietness of sweet sounds.

The house, set on a hill, commanded panoramic views over banana groves meandering out to the blue sea beyond. This morning, the white-capped peaks of Tenerife were clearly visible across the miles of sparkling water.

The beauty of it all caught at Joanna's throat as, clad in blue denim shorts and a sleeveless top, she walked on to the terrace on long golden legs to shake back a silky curtain of brown hair and lift her face to the sun. The casual, graceful gesture gave the falling line of her profile a swift, vivid loveliness.

Turning her head a little to her left, she could see the beautiful Spanish villa just visible as it towered disdainfully aloft among the trees. It was the residence of the Marquéls Ramón de Orleron y Faustino who was a pet as well as being monarch of all he surveyed. He was immensely rich with a family tree that could be traced back for hundreds of years and, like his residence of tall windows, carved stone pediments and famous gardens, he was just as nobly handsome. He owned most of the island, including the house Joanna's father rented from him.

'So you are up, Miss Joanna.'

Rosita who, with her husband Jaime, had been at the Villa Rosario for most of Joanna's nineteen years, waddled on to the terrace with the breakfast tray. She was a buxom woman in her forties with black hair and dark flashing eyes who had a passion for bright colours. The button-through cotton dress in shocking pink hugging her ample figure gave her the appearance of a huge poinsettia on two thick brown stalks of legs as she laid the tray down on the white wicker table.

Joanna drew up a chair. 'Lovely morning,' she said, reaching for the glass of iced fruit juice. 'Has Daddy gone to Las Palmas?'

'He has.' Rosita emptied the tray and glowered fiercely. 'It's going to be another hot day, so take that sombrero with you when you go gallivanting this morning.' The dark eyes glowered at Joanna's youthful slimness. 'Here I go trying to feed you out into curves and you just let that old sun dehydrate you into a stick of sugar cane. That's all you is no matter how I try to feed you up.'

The first drink of fruit juice was delicious to Joanna, who felt as if the golden morning was cruising down her throat. 'I'm sorry, Rosita,' she said, 'but we Mains never seem to put on weight. I'm like Daddy in that respect. But I'm sure you love us as we are.' Her tawny eyes danced with mischief. 'Not to worry. After all, there are all kinds of beauty aids on the market today. Things like ... er ... false busts ...'

Her voice trailed off into a chuckle of laughter, but Rosita was not amused. She looked at Joanna darkly before ambling away with a snort and Joanna blew kisses at her broad pink back. Just for that, she thought gleefully, I shall be packed off with a lunch large enough to satisfy a horse. Rosita was a dear, and so protective to her ewe lamb that Joanna could never resist teasing her. Her husband Jaime was as docile as she was fiery. They had been blessed with three children who were now away at university through the generosity of Nick Main, and now they devoted their life to their benefactor and his motherless daughter Joanna.

Joanna had been four years old when her mother had died rather suddenly at their home in London and her father, unable to settle after her death, had sold up and gone to live in the Canary islands. Joanna, pale and wan and missing her mother dreadfully, had bloomed like a flower in the sun and gradually the beauty of her surroundings had sought expression in her love to draw and paint. An interest that had grown through the years had become serious and she lived to paint. There was so much beauty on the island —the soft-eyed donkeys with their burdens, the workers on the banana plantations reaching almost to the cliff tops, the many flowers and shrubs and the hill scenes of caves made into dwellings as sweet and inviting as any English cottage.

Against the whitewashed entrances the vivid splash of scarlet geraniums in hanging baskets was as picturesque and breathtaking as the panoramic views commanded from these strongholds. Indeed the views were as grand as those from the villa of the Marqués which brought Joanna's thoughts to the work in hand. Her latest painting was of his lovely Spanish villa to which she was about to add the finishing touches.

After breakfast she set off on her pony with her paints, canvas and lunch, plus the sombrero which Rosita insisted upon her wearing and made for the hills.

Joanna loved the hills with their strange mingling of simplicity and barbarity drenched in flowers whose colours vibrated against purple shadows of cypress and poplar. In the intensity of an immense blue sky there was a zest for living, a consciousness of tranquillity and freshness as one breathed in air like wine. The way grew steeper and Joanna called gaily to a man on a donkey going downwards to the village below.

At last they climbed to a grassy hollow where the Spanish villa of the Marqués was clearly visible in its entirety. Here, Joanna dismounted and put the pony out to grass. Then setting up her easel, she sorted out her paints. The villa of the Marqués, Las Jacarandas, was a twin-belfreyed, white-porticoed building with a terrace of white columns and an entrance porch where trellises of vines gave shade from the fierceness of the sun. Behind the big white villa were other buildings including stables all of which were set in magnificent grounds of statuary and fountains and rolling green lawns in between shrubbery and magnificent trees.

There was almost a profound silence broken only by sweet sounds, the tinkle of a goat bell and a voice calling from far away. Tenderly, Joanna touched up the red and white hibiscus visible behind the iron grilles of Las Jacarandas and leaned back to see the desired effect against the white walls. It really was a beautiful villa and she could never do justice to it, but the result was pleasing even to her critical eye. The Marqués would, no doubt, be more critical than she was, seeing that he had a wonderful collection of old masters gracing his lovely villa. He was also a man of experience, and wise beyond his thirty-one years.

He was also a clever chess player and a very great friend of her father. Joanna was no mean hand at chess herself, but she could never beat the Marqués. Anxiously, she surveyed the now completed picture searching for flaws, flaws which, she knew, would be spotted immediately by the keen dark eyes of the Marqués. Perhaps a little more white in the blue sky, a little more purple in the shadows? With her head on one side Joanna pondered, then resigned herself to the finished product: If he did not like it then it was just too bad. After all, it would probably be the only picture he would have for his birthday. And it was really lovely, even though she thought so herself.

She ate her lunch—tortilla, fruit and drank the *tinto*, the local Canary wine, and proceeded to take out of the saddle bag a button-through dress in cream, trimmed in red, to wear over her shorts. Shorts were not looked on with favour, especially when entering churches and one held the same respect for people like the Marqués who also held up the tradition of moderation in clothing. Slacks and shorts were allowed on the beaches, but one usually donned a bathing wrap or sun-dress to sit about.

The painting was dry when she packed it up along with the rest of her paraphernalia and mounted the pony. The wide, heavy door was open into the entrance of Las Jacarandas, the interior cool and dark after the heat of the sun. Inside the villa one became quickly accustomed to the sense of coolness and space and the evidence of wealth. The exquisite workmanship of the carved staircase and tall windows were at one with the magnificent views outside. Priceless carpets covered the floors and graceful furniture gave a dignity to white walls.

'*Buenas tardes, señorita.* The Señor Marqués awaits you in the *salón*. Mateo will take care of your pony.' Andrés, the uniformed manservant, appeared before her, politely courteous, and stepped aside for her to precede him into the villa.

Joanna, holding the picture, crossed the hall to enter a *salón* beneath a Moorish archway. At once her host came forward to greet her. Like the people of Las Palmas, the Marqués tended to be rather taller than the average, with a somewhat lighter skin and definite shades of red in the crisp dark hair. His white smile was only one of his undoubted charms. There was a masculine jut to his nose and he had a beautiful mouth. In the muted light filtering through the tall windows, the clean-cut, arrogant features were even more striking than usual, the smooth olive skin flatteringly darker.

'*Buenas tardes*, Juana,' he exclaimed, using his pet name for her. 'Do come and sit down. You should not be out in this heat.'

He strode across the *salón* and drew her forward. But she drew back, and offered him the painting. 'Your birthday present from me,' she said somewhat tentatively, and pushed the canvas into his hands.

There was a long moment of silence as he accepted the gift and, lifting it in long, slim brown hands, studied it with complete absorption. Joanna's tawny eyes surveyed him thoughtfully, taking in the vivid silk scarf tucked into the open-necked shirt, the immaculate slacks and the spotless white doeskin shoes. She was a prey to conflicting emotions at the quizzical smile which lightened his eyes before his lips followed suit.

Why did he not say something? Was it that bad? Surely not? His eyes were glued to the canvas. The thought that he had no wish to meet the frankness of her eyes when delivering his verdict dyed her cheeks a deep red, and rendered her momentarily speechless. At last, she could bear the suspense no longer. In a voice no louder than a whisper, she asked tentatively,

'Don't you like it, Ramón?'

'Like it?' He shook his head as if amazed at his own good fortune in being the recipient of such a gift. 'You know, my Juana,' he answered with his eyes still intent upon the picture, 'when your father told me of your desire to paint I never imagined results such as this. It is magnificent. I must arrange an exhibition for you in Las Palmas. Who knows? One day you could become as famous as your father.' He smiled down into her tense little face. The cord around her neck was still holding the sombrero which had slipped down her back, leaving her looking young and defenceless. He ruffled her hair. 'You would like that?'

Her blush deepened under his regard. 'One famous name in the family is enough,' she assured him firmly. 'I am quite happy to know that you like it. If you don't, I can give you something else.'

He looked down at her then, almost as long as he had looked at the painting. Then he said slowly, 'Thank you, Juana, for this very precious gift. I shall treasure it all my life. And now,' he put the picture down gently against the wall and his long fingers reached out to the cord at her neck, 'let us untie this sombrero before it strangles you. Then we can take refreshment.'

Andrés brought in refreshment and Joanna swallowed her drink thirstily while Ramón leaned back against a table and regarded her with some amusement.

'So you have no desire for publicity, Juana. Why not? It is time you began to circulate more freely into society. Have you no wish to travel, to see the world, to go to England?' he probed politely.

Joanna sighed and whirled the ice cubes round in her glass. 'I've always wanted to go to England, but you know Daddy hasn't gone back since Mummy died. He says he can't bear to go back to places he knew with her.'

'One can understand that,' he conceded. 'This desire of yours to go back to your birthplace, does it mean that some day you plan on returning there to live?'

She shook her head. 'I don't know. I'm very happy here but Daddy has fed me on so much English literature that I feel I belong there more than here. And Daddy has all his English friends coming to the villa from time to time. Do you know that he has gone to Las Palmas this morning to meet two people who are playing the lead in his new play due to open in London?'

He raised a dark brow. 'Sounds interesting. I shall have to invite them to dinner along with you and your father.'

She laughed, completely at ease with him. 'That will be nice,' she said, the laughter bubbling up in her tawny eyes.

Ramón's dark eyes wandered slowly over the young vital face, free from make-up, and paused on the shiny brown hair. He had watched her growing gently into her teens and filling out rather slowly in all the right places. She was young, sweet and utterly untouched. He prayed that she would stay that way.

He replenished her cup and went on to talk of other things. When she took her leave, he watched her go, then went indoors and, picking up the picture, became once again absorbed in it.

The visitors had arrived when she reached the Villa Rosario. Joanna stabled the pony and crossed the courtyard in the direction that the voices were coming from. Passing the paw-paw tree and the Indian laurel, she skirted the begonias and walked on to the verandah. Her father was there, in worsted trousers and open-necked shirt, a young-looking man of forty-two with neat brown hair and a Van Dyck beard, precision-cut. Next to him, her lovely limbs stretched out on a lounger, was a beautiful blonde. The sun sprayed gold dust in her hair and her eyes were sky blue.

'Hello,' she said on a dazzling smile. 'You must be Joanna. I'm Candida Marshall. Pleased to meet you.'

She held out a limp hand and Joanna took it. 'I like your name,' she admitted frankly.

Candida laughed, a pleased laugh as husky as her voice. 'I'm going to like your daughter, Nick,' she cooed.

The third person was standing with his back to the

verandah wall. He wore an open-necked shirt and cream slacks and his hair was fair with a stray lock hanging over his dark grey eyes. His mobile mouth lifted at the corners as he stared intently at her. Then he lunged from the wall, stepped forward and proffered a masculine hand. 'Hello, Joanna,' he said. 'I'm Laurence Nesbit.'

Joanna blinked. He was so utterly English that she could almost hear Big Ben strike. She gave herself a little shake and answered cordially.

CHAPTER TWO

NICK took his visitors into Las Palmas for the evening along with Joanna. While they dined they were serenaded by a romantic Spaniard with a drooping moustache and a guitar. They all enjoyed themselves immensely. Joanna was surprised to find Candida and Laurence settling down so well. They went on a tour of the banana estates and picked up enough Spanish to share a joke with the workers. Rosita liked them too, especially Laurence, whose deep brown voice could wheedle the ducks off the water.

Ramón called one morning to remind them of the dinner he was giving that evening on the event of his birthday. He strode on to the verandah where they were all having breakfast. The spare, clean-cut look of him, his air of distinction captured the interest of Candida. Her greeting, however, was skilfully casual as Nick introduced them.

Ramón bowed, his dark eyes caught in the torch-like beam of sun sending sparks from Candida's golden hair. 'Welcome to our island,' he said, and turned to Nick. 'I have come to remind you about this evening. Dinner is at seven-thirty. I want you all to come.' His dark eyes moved over the four faces turned in his direction. 'There will be quite a crowd and I am sure you will enjoy yourselves.'

Nick said warmly, 'We always do at your parties, Ramón. We are lucky to be included in your friends.'

Joanna gave Ramón her warm smile. Against the fair colouring of Laurence, he appeared to be very foreign this morning. His immaculate white breeches and the white silk shirt open on a strong smooth brown throat accentuated the liquid dark eyes and the strong planes of his tanned face.

'And what of Nick Main, celebrated author and playwright? Should I not feel honoured to be counted among his friends?' Ramón teased.

Nick answered on the expressive elevation of an eyebrow. 'I'm only doing a job which I'm sure you would be just as good at, even better, if you decided to write. We shall be delighted to accept your invitation. We plan to rehearse the play each morning and relax for the rest of the day.'

'Until this evening, then. *Adios*.'

Ramón bent his head to include all present, then he turned and strode from the verandah.

Candida was the first to speak when he had gone. 'Now there's a man who could make a fortune on the films and stage. He has good looks, breeding, a compelling charm and a voice that sends goose pimples all over me. I can't wait until tonight. Where does this Adonis hang out?'

She looked askance at Nick, who waved a hand in the direction of the hills.

'There you see up among the greenery Las Jacarandas, home of the Marqués Ramón de Orleron y Faustino. He owns this house and anywhere else you care to gaze on from this verandah.'

Candida digested this, then said, 'Why do Spaniards always have such long names?'

'Because their mother's name comes first, then their father's,' Nick replied.

Candida shrugged. 'It certainly sounds very impressive, but the Marqués would be just as disturbing if his name was Smith. I'm beginning to grow very fond of your island, or should I say the Marqués's?'

She went into Joanna's room that evening looking very lovely in a halter-necked dress of black silk chiffon. The diamond clasp fastening the four ropes of pearls around her throat matched the clasp in the front of her fair chignon of hair. Her eyelids were a faint shade of blue and her lips were the same kind of pink as her nails. She looked with appraisal at Joanna's dress, a full-skirted cream silk edged with a band of blue flowers which fitted snugly in at her small waist. The brown hair was a swinging curtain of silk with gold lights in it. She looked fresh, young and sweet.

Candida said with a small crooked smile on her lovely

lips, 'You look awfully young, Joanna, and very pretty.'

Joanna smiled. 'Thanks. I'm all of nineteen.'

'I'm twenty-six.' Candida perched on the arm of a chair, her blue eyes dark with an emotion Joanna could not define. 'I suppose,' she went on, studying her beautifully manicured nails, 'the Marqués entertains frequently.'

'Yes, he does.'

'And he isn't married?'

'No. He's a darling.'

'Are you in love with him, Joanna?' Candida's gesture of a slim hand was vaguely apologetic. 'I don't mean to pry, but your face lights up when you speak of him, and he is one of the most fabulous men I have ever met.'

'I've never thought of Ramón in that way,' Joanna admitted with such honesty that Candida's eyes widened.

'You're sure of that?' she asked as though she could not believe it.

Joanna shook her head. 'Ramón is our very good friend.' She bit her lip and frowned. 'I . . . like him very much——' she began.

'Enough to marry him if he asked you?'

'Good heavens, no! You don't marry a man because you happen to be fond of him. You have to love him very much and he has to love you in the same way. At least, that's what I think,' Joanna said firmly.

Candida's smile was awry. 'Don't you want to get married, Joanna?'

'Of course. Every girl does. Don't you, or are you already married?'

Candida laughed and displayed her ringless hands. 'No. You're bright, aren't you?'

Joanna blushed furiously and picked up her evening bag. 'I only thought that you might be because you're so beautiful and feminine.'

'I've had my moments and my men,' Candida admitted with brutal frankness. 'Nothing came of any of my affairs. Don't get me wrong—I've never slept with a man to further my career. I've always been so sure that one day my name will be up in lights through my own efforts. Success would mean nothing to me if I hadn't earned it. I'm hoping this play of Nick's is my passport to fame.'

'Isn't that rather risky, sleeping around with men? If I did that I'd become so confused, I wouldn't know the right man when he came along.' Joanna played with the clasp of her evening bag. 'Ramón is no monk, you know. He's had affairs.'

'You don't need to tell me that. It makes him all the more exciting. Most attractive men have affairs before they are married. The women won't leave them alone,' Candida mocked.

'Do the women run after Laurence?'

'Of course they do. Mind you, he's an unknown yet as an actor, like me. Laurence is a nice fellow, like your Ramón.' Candida's eyes went hard. 'Do you mind if I make a play for the Marqués? I might fall in love with his sterling qualities. I'm half in love with his looks already.'

Joanna stared on a soundless gasp and Candida gave her a sardonic look.

'But what about your part in the play?' she asked weakly.

Candida stood up and smoothed out the skirt of her dress. 'I'm after two things, fame and a husband.'

'But Ramón lives here in the Islands. He isn't the kind of man who would agree to you carrying on with your career.' Joanna's bottom lip trembled a little. 'He will want children to inherit his title and his possessions.'

Candida strolled towards the door. 'And why do you think I want a husband if it wasn't for those things? Oh, I've met lots of men, some with titles and nothing else, and all they were interested in was having a good time. It certainly looks as though Ramón is the man I've been waiting for. You see, I'm calling him Ramón already.' Again her voice held that trace of mockery, and Joanna could not make up her mind whether she was only teasing or in earnest. She could not think of a word to say as she walked with her companion to the door. Candida patted her arm. 'Don't worry, your Ramón will be hard to get—of that I'm sure. But it's worth a try. I had to tell you first because I'm not sure now whether you will mind.'

Joanna smiled. 'I don't mind so long as you do really fall in love with him. I wouldn't want Ramón to have a wife who wanted him just for a home and children.' They had reached the door and she looked right into the enigmatic blue eyes. 'Why are you telling me this?' she asked quietly.

Candida met her gaze squarely. 'Because Nick is giving me a chance that many actresses would give their all for. I couldn't very well hurt his daughter, could I? Besides, I always like to play fair. It's the only way to reap a fair reward. Anyway, I like you.'

She thrust an arm through Joanna's and they walked downstairs to where Nick and Laurence awaited. Both men looked distinguished in evening dress and Joanna was rewarded by a look of appraisal from the dark grey eyes of Laurence.

Nick took the wheel of the car with Laurence sitting beside him. Joanna sat immediately behind Laurence and gazed at his broad shoulders, admiring the fair curling hair in the nape of his neck. Candida, sitting beside her, was saying, 'I find the sharp contrasts of dazzling light and fierce shadows get me, along with the dazzling flora of bougainvillaea, hibiscus, oleander and mimosa. You certainly have a paradise of a place, Nick. I can understand you not wanting to come back to London.'

Nick said, 'Don't forget I'm a writer who likes quiet and I'm not the gregarious type. This place suits me because I work too hard to become bored in any way. You might find it beginning to pall within six months. One can have too much sun.'

'Whoever heard of anybody being bored living in Paradise?' put in Laurence lazily. 'If I'm a success in your play, Nick, I'm going to buy myself a villa here.'

'And I'll be your first guest,' Candida promised as she gazed out dreamily on banana plantations reaching for the cliff tops where white dwellings clung to the slopes.

Joanna knew her companion was relishing the grandeur and beauty of it all. But, like Nick, she wondered how long the island would hold Candida when the novelty had worn off. Like all lovely women she was used to her quota of admiring glances. It was a part of her everyday life. Life on the island was limited. If Joanna had sensed her own isolation she had escaped from it of her own accord. The beauty of it fascinated and intoxicated her. If she had thought the grounds and views from the Villa Rosario exquisite, she was spellbound by Las Jacarandas. Here nothing was quite real; nothing impossible.

Whereas she always took the mountain road to the villa of the Marqués when on her pony, her father was taking them the long way round through the village. The village square was enchanting, bordered on one side by an imposing palace and on the other by a splendid cathedral. Then the village was left behind and the road meandered upwards between rich green folds and soon the twin towers of Las Jacarandas were to be seen among the trees. It was a breathtaking scene of beauty beneath a dazzling blue sky. The enormous surrounding trees gave the villa a fairy tale setting and Candida sat up in frank admiration.

'This is nice,' she exclaimed somewhat inadequately, and seemed lost for words as Nick swung the car round on an avenue bordered by superb trees. The bower of greenery seemed to go on forever. Then suddenly the road had resolved itself into a garden, a heartrendingly beautiful Arabian garden brilliant with magnolias, oleanders and bougainvillaea with crimson blossom. The car turned smoothly along a curve in the drive, making scarcely a sound on the red earth, and drew up at the main entrance of Las Jacarandas. It was a mammoth residence with twin towers spreading itself over elegant velvet lawns. Deep awnings protected the windows and terraces from the dazzle of the sun and a brilliant bougainvillaea climbed over the entrance to shed a shower of blossom.

Ramón was waiting for them, very much the Marqués in his white dinner jacket. He was tall, smiling and charming. He was all glow, with a vital kinetic magnetism which was a congenital part of his make-up. Greeting them with consummate ease, he ushered them indoors to the cool beauty of silky Persian rugs on the polished hall floor and escorted them past furniture and pedestals incredibly lovely in shape and design to the main *salón*.

Joanna looked about her as they entered the *salón*. She had grown accustomed to the luxurious status of Las Jacarandas, but now, walking beside Candida, she was inclined to see it anew through her surprised blue eyes.

There was an aura of richness in the air, the perfume of expensive cigars, expensive wine, expensive perfume and the gleam of jewelled dresses. The guests already assembled looked brown and fit, the men elegant in evening dress, the women in fabulous dresses each as expensive as the other. Ramón introduced Candida and Laurence, and Joanna, accompanied by her father, mingled with the guests they already knew. Waiters skimmed about at speed serving wine and everyone was relaxed and smiling.

The dinner which followed was perfection, and later there was dancing. Coffee had been served on the terrace in the warm golden glow of a summer evening. Then the guests left the terrace, crossed the wide hallway to where double doors had been flung open to the ballroom. It was a long room with a bar at one end and small tables and chairs against the walls. The lighting was ingeniously done, to give soft pools of golden light, and Candida's blonde hair gleamed in an incredibly rich gold, Joanna noticed, as she was approached by Ramón for a dance.

The small band of musicians, who were playing on a small dais in a corner, struck up a number and Ramón moved off with Candida in his arms. Watching them, Joanna tried to analyse the way she felt at the sight of them. She had seen Ramón dozens of times with beautiful women in his arms and he had danced smoothly with his face in the usual enigmatic lines. This time he looked no different, but Candida's face was not far below his dark one, for she was tall and their lips could have met easily with very little effort on her part. Did she resent Candida now that she knew what her intentions were towards Ramón? She began to wish that Candida had not said anything. Whatever happened Ramón would always be her very good friend, even if he took a wife. The mixed emotions that the sight of the golden head so near to the black one conjured up inside her were not only indefinable but far from pleasant. Indeed, something like a shadow flitted over the pleasure of her evening.

'May I have the pleasure?'

With a little start she turned her head to see Laurence smiling down at her. He took her hand and the next moment his arms were around her and they were moving away on the dance floor in perfect rhythm. Soon Ramón was forgotten as Joanna gave herself up to the pleasure of the dance. Laurence was an accomplished dancer and Joanna loved to dance.

'You're looking very lovely,' Laurence murmured above her hair. 'I love those streaky lines in your hair. It's like silk.'

A dimple appeared in her cheek. 'I bet you say that to all the girls. My hair is mousy, streaks and all.' Joanna lifted her face and her soft hair swung softly against her shoulders. 'I like your hair better. I like the way it curls in your neck at the back.'

Laurence looked down at her thoughtfully. 'I've never met anyone like you before. You're like a little brown elf who has slid down a sunbeam into my arms. There's something so refreshingly untouched and lovely about you. And you're so natural.' He smiled ruefully, 'I don't know if it's the atmosphere of the island that makes one feel romantic, but unless I'm very much mistaken, I'm going to like you more than a little. You don't mind?'

His dark grey eyes searched her tawny ones soberly. 'Why should I? You and I are going to have lots of fun,' she answered. And they did, teasing each other, dancing and laughing and eventually sitting at the bar where Joanna went into convulsions of laughter when she tried to teach him more about the Spanish language and food. And through it all Laurence smiled and looked at her tenderly, and Joanna, blushing under that look, told herself that life with a big, blond Englishman with his hair curling deliciously in the nape of his neck could be very exciting indeed.

The following morning while Candida, Laurence and Nick were going through his play, Joanna decided to make one of her rare trips into Las Palmas to restock her paints. She drove the twenty odd miles in Nick's big car because he wanted it servicing at a garage there. One of the numerous banana trucks making their daily journeys into Las Palmas to the docks would give her a lift back. She left the car at the garage, bought her paints among other purchases and had a coffee. She had a nice morning, and made her way down to the harbour to the banana trucks unloading on the quay.

The South African mail boat had arrived that morning and there was still plenty of activity. Most of the passengers had already disembarked and the unloading of freight was now in progress. Joanna could see several green trucks belonging to the Marqués waiting to shed their load. Any of the drivers would be pleased to give her a lift back, so she sat down on the low harbour wall to wait. As usual most of the inhabitants of Las Palmas had come down to greet the ship, and there, apart yet very much one of the crowd, was Ramón. He stood leaning back elegantly against a pile of packing cases, his dark eyes fixed on the big white ship. He wore the usual correctly tied silk scarf in the open-necked shirt above immaculate cream slacks, and his dark hair, springing back crisply from his forehead, had the black of a raven's plumage in the sun. There was a latent strength about his hard-muscled frame and a suggestion that he could shed that deceptive lazy attitude and spring forward at the drop of a hat. It was not only that he was so very handsome, he was also extremely intelligent and terribly nice.

He was evidently waiting for some mail from the ship, for he glanced at his wrist watch. Maybe he was just the man for Candida after all. It would have been flattering if he had had just the teeniest little crush on herself, though, Joanna thought wistfully. She was sure that beautifully firm mouth of his could kiss quite thrillingly and he would, no doubt, make love charmingly too. She noticed three pretty girls in flowered dresses standing near him. They were trying in vain to attract his attention by raising their voices in conversation with each other and sending coy glances accompanied by rather shrill laughter his way.

Joanna was congratulating herself on seeing him, for it meant a lift back home in his luxurious car instead of a banana truck, a ride with the bumpy roads cushioned by deep springs and the coolness of rich leather. He saw her as he went forward towards the ship and lifted a hand in greeting before springing up the gangway to greet the captain waiting at the top. He was down again in minutes carrying several large flat parcels beneath his arm and he strode to where she now stood waiting by the harbour wall.

For long moments his brilliant dark gaze took in the white sleeveless dress and moved slowly to where the brilliance of the sun was striking lights from her brown hair minus the sombrero. One slim hand held a shopping bag filled with her purchases and their eyes encountered with a little tingling shock which startled her though it had gone in a flash.

'Juana,' he demanded, eagle-eyed, 'what are you doing here? Are you waiting for something off the boat?'

She lowered her lashes demurely. 'I was hoping for a lift in one of your trucks back to the Villa Rosario,' she answered.

Ramón looked startled and annoyed. His lips thinned. 'How did you arrive here? Not in one of my trucks, I trust?'

'No,' Joanna answered placatingly. 'I brought Daddy's car to the garage to be serviced. It won't be ready today, so it was either the bus or one of your trucks.'

'Indeed?' Grimly, Ramón reached for her shopping bag, relieved her of it, and putting firm fingers beneath her elbow escorted her to where he had parked his car. There he deposited his parcels and the shopping bag in the car boot and helped her into the front seat. Eyeing him thoughtfully as he slid into the driving seat beside her, Joanna decided that he was more than preoccupied with his own thoughts. His clear-cut arrogant profile was set and one lean hard finger jabbed the starter rather viciously.

'It was a bit of luck seeing you,' she said after he had

backed the car out of the parking space and set it forward at speed.

He did not appear to have heard her, for he drove for some distance to set the car purring up an incline as they left the harbour far behind before he spoke.

'You were saying?' he prompted, cocking an inquiring brow.

Her gaze swept from the wine-coloured silk scarf tucked into his open-necked shirt down to his well shod feet. He would be meeting Candida again soon, she knew. No doubt she was to spend the afternoon with him and the evening too. He was preoccupied all right, thinking of hair like spun gold and eyes as blue as the sky overhead.

'Nothing,' she answered shortly, and felt like hitting him.

The air of camaraderie which usually existed between them was absent. Ramón's voice was that of a stranger. 'I shall have to have a talk with your father,' he said in clipped tones, while giving attention to his driving. 'He does not concern himself with you enough. You need protection. In the future I forbid you to drive in any of my trucks, and I shall instruct my drivers to that effect.'

Joanna looked at him in dismay. Most of the truck drivers were old friends and there was always plenty of fun to be had on the way through the teasing and joking that went on on both sides.

'But why?' she insisted.

With controlled exasperation, Ramón answered, 'Because it does not become you, Juana. You are no longer a child, and your pride alone, not to mention your dignity, should make you aware that such a thing is not done by well brought up young women. If you will not take heed of my wishes for yourself, will you do it for my sake?'

Joanna stared. The arrogant Marqués being humble! She could not believe it. And in some way it hurt her. Had Candida something to do with his new approach, which was altogether out of character? She had never known him ask anything before. He had always been very much the Marqués, whose wishes were his command.

'But we are English, Ramón,' she remonstrated gently.

'We are more tolerant and not so demanding.'

'And what do you mean by that?'

His voice had slid on ice and Joanna sought around for oil to pour on the troubled waters. The thought of falling out with her beloved Ramón was not to be endured.

'What you need is a wife to fuss over,' she said with conviction. 'You aren't getting any younger.' And as Ramón —who had only just left his twenties—grinned at this thrust, she hurried on, 'A man in your position needs a wife.'

He raised an appreciative brow. 'A little trite,' he observed. 'But true enough.' There was a pause, then he added, 'Have you anyone in mind?'

'There are so many for you to choose from among your many friends, and your relations would be delighted,' she hastened to assure him.

Ramón looked thoughtful. 'Am I not the one to be delighted?' he demanded.

'You will be if you let yourself fall in love.'

'So, I fall in love first?'

She laughed and met his dark swift look with dancing eyes. 'Oh, Ramón, you're teasing! Perhaps it isn't essential for you to fall in love. You Spaniards do things differently from us.'

He looked startled. 'Strange, I had the impression that love was the same the world over. Have you ever been in love, Juana?'

She shook her head, looking deliciously uncomplicated. 'No. But I shall be some day.' She put her head on one side consideringly. 'I rather think it will be an Englishman like Daddy. I adore him.'

His voice suddenly rasped. 'Your father's type is far too old for you. You do not know a thing about it. Furthermore, you are just the kind of little idiot to go after a man twice your age. If you were my daughter . . .'

'Yes?' Joanna twinkled at him. 'Go on, what would you do? Do tell me.' Suddenly she burst into a quiet peal of laughter. 'What are we talking about? You're not old enough to be my father. Oh, Ramón, you are funny!'

He was not amused. But he said no more. He dropped

her off at the Villa Rosario and sped away with a brief smile and a still briefer '*Adios*.'

Going into the villa swinging her shopping bag, Joanna wondered what could have been the matter with him. Poor Ramón! He was evidently in love with Candida, and the dear that he was, he had fallen harder than most.

Everyone was in a good humour at lunch time. The rehearsal of the play had gone well and Nick was pleased with the progress they were making. Candida, looking very lovely in a housecoat of delicate lavender which deepened the blue of her eyes, ate a hearty lunch, then hurried away to dress for an afternoon with Ramón. He sent Andrés in his car to pick her up and Joanna heard her go while she was in the kitchen picking up a picnic tea from Rosita.

'Goodness, Rosita,' she exclaimed on seeing the amount of food being prepared, 'surely all that isn't for us? It isn't the army going on manoeuvres. It's only Laurence and me.'

Rosita rammed the last pile of food into the picnic hamper and said firmly,

'Young people are always hungry and Laurence has a lot of space to fill. You also.' She looked darkly at Joanna's willowy figure. 'See that you eat your share, and no more talk of wearing false busts. The best padding I know and the healthiest is good food. And take that sombrero!'

The last few words were shouted at Joanna's retreating back, and Rosita with a shake of her head continued with the task in hand. Laurence borrowed Nick's pony and Joanna led the way to her favourite spot in the hills on hers.

She had taken her painting paraphernalia along with an extra canvas for Laurence, who boasted that he used to be pretty good at art when at school. It was a beautiful day and they rode up to the grassy plateau where she had painted the villa of the Marqués.

'Isn't that Las Jacarandas over there?' said Laurence, squinting against the glare of the sun to the twin turrets of the villa among the trees.

Joanna set up his easel and one for herself. Somehow the lovely white building dreaming in the sun had lost its magic this afternoon with the thought of Candida being there.

'It is,' she answered, more lighthearted than she felt. 'Nice place, isn't it? Did you enjoy your visit last evening?'

'Rather. Quite a guy, isn't he? Candida seems to be interested—but then what woman could ask for more? I'm surprised you haven't snapped him up yourself. I'm glad you haven't, though. I wouldn't be here with you now if you had. He isn't the kind to let his wife go on picnics with other men.'

Joanna laughed. 'What man worth his salt would do?'

Laurence let this pass and drew his easel near to the clump of rock that was to be his seat. For the next half hour or so there was silence between them as they became engrossed in their work. It was Laurence who gave up first, throwing down his brushes and stretching out his long arms on a yawn.

'I don't know about you,' he said, 'but I feel partial to a drink. Anything handy?' He strolled over to where Joanna was sitting and looked down at her canvas. 'Isn't that Candida?'

Joanna shone up at him. 'You recognised her?' she exclaimed with delight. 'You really think it's a good likeness?'

He nodded and his eyes narrowed on her effulgent face. 'A remarkable likeness, especially since you don't dabble in portraits. Why Candida?'

She shook her head and looked at the portrait bewilderedly. 'I don't know. I hadn't decided what to paint and it just happened.'

Laurence smiled and patted her head. 'You don't have to apologise for doing a good portrait. It's only . . .'

He paused and she looked up at him curiously. 'Only what?' she demanded.

He pushed his hands into the pockets of his slacks and said moodily,

'Come and look at my canvas and you'll see what I mean.'

Joanna rose to her feet and walked over to his easel. The next moment her eyes had widened to the full extent with wonder and admiration. She was staring at a profile of herself.

'It's beautiful, Laurence,' she breathed. 'Why, you're quite good. In fact you're marvellous. Why me?' She turned to look up at his serious face.

'Like your portrait of Candida, it just happened. It does, you know, when you have someone on your mind.'

She frowned. 'I don't know what you mean. I hadn't got Candida on my mind.'

He said heavily, 'You probably had the Marqués on your mind, because she's there with him this afternoon.'

Joanna stared aghast. 'Why should you think that? Ramón is just a friend. Besides, it's no business of yours.'

Laurence went a dull red beneath his tan and rubbed his clean-shaven chin sheepishly. 'I'm sorry,' he said apologetically. 'It really isn't any of my business. But you must admit that you are very fond of the Marqués, and he is a charming man, very likeable.'

Joanna looked at his downcast face and impulsively laid a comforting hand on his arm. 'I'm sorry too for being so sharp. I didn't mean to be. You see, Laurence, you aren't the only one who has accused me of being in love with Ramón. Candida has too. He is a very attractive, charming man. Furthermore, he's so terribly nice. I suppose . . .' her laugh was a trifle self-conscious, 'well, I am very fond of him, but as for being in love with him—goodness, you can be fond of a person, you know, as a friend.' She smiled up at him. 'Come on, have that drink you're wanting so badly and then we'll eat.'

They sat down in the grassy hollow and Joanna brought out a can of beer for Laurence. Then they proceeded to eat the packed meal which Rosita had so generously provided—delicious omelettes, Spanish style, with large quantities of cold meat and fruit. It was after they had eaten and were drinking coffee poured steaming from a flask that Laurence put on a cigarette and stretched his long length out contentedly.

'This is just what the doctor ordered,' he mused, eyes closed as he leaned back against a rock. 'We must do this again.'

Joanna's eyes were drawn to his rugged profile and

noticed that the hand holding the cigarette was thickly fashioned, the fingers short and spatulate. They were, she thought, the hands of a man with considerable imagination and ability. A lock of fair hair tended to flop down on his forehead which he flicked back occasionally, and she found the gesture, along with his deep cultured voice, curiously attractive. And he was English. This, of course, was of paramount importance to Joanna.

'Have you any family, Laurence?' she asked shyly.

He opened an eye and glanced at her before closing it again. He said, 'My parents live in Buckinghamshire. Dad farms a sizeable tract of land, wanted me to be a farmer. I wanted to act, so we made a bargain. If I don't make good in five years, I'll go back on the farm. This is my first break in three years of small parts in rep.'

Joanna looked out on hills where goats moved in their grazing and the occasional colourful figure of a gypsy searching for thick strands of grass for weaving lent colour of movement. Her serenity gave her brown-haired, fragile appearance a touching quality.

She said wistfully, 'Tell me about England. I remember very little of it in the few short years I was there.'

CHAPTER THREE

JOANNA did not sleep very well that night. The next morning she went down to the beach for a swim and came back feeling unrefreshed. At breakfast, her companions were bright enough. Nick was busy reading his mail and Candida was full of sparkle and ready for gossip. Apparently she had enjoyed her second visit to Las Jacarandas and was going out with Ramón that afternoon. She was highly amused to hear from Laurence that Joanna had painted her portrait.

'How exciting,' she said. 'No one has ever painted my picture before. I just can't wait to see it.'

Joanna blushed and said, 'It isn't very good, I'm afraid.'

'It's extremely good,' Laurence contradicted stoutly.

Both Nick and Candida agreed with him when Joanna fetched the canvas for them to see.

'Let me buy it,' Candida pleaded. 'I think it's beautiful.'

'You can have it,' Joanna said generously. 'I'm glad you like it.'

Candida was enchanted. 'You ought to take up portrait painting. I'm sure you would be a success.'

Joanna made no reply. At the moment even her interest in painting had diminished. And the trouble was, she had no reason for it. That afternoon she went out with Laurence into Las Palmas. Her outings with him took on a very different aspect from those with Nick or Ramón. With Laurence she felt more like a tourist going to all the places that normally she would never enter, like little gift shops and roadside cafés. They laughed and joked a great deal, especially when Laurence chose to do absurd things like buying a couple of tourists' sombreros which he insisted upon them both wearing on their tour of the town. Everything had been fine until she took him to the Spanish Club for drinks. The members were mostly composed of an exclusive set of residents, of which Nick and Ramón were members, along with herself.

Ramón had to be there, seated elegantly at a table with Candida, who was apparently succumbing to his undoubted charm. Her golden hair was even more striking than usual and her peach skin was flatteringly golden with the new tan.

She was chattering away to Ramón, who had one eyebrow raised provocatively. He was smiling and he was easily the handsomest man in the room. Joanna wanted to turn tail and run, regretting her impulse to take Laurence there for an iced drink. The day was hot and it was cool in the club. The service too was excellent and the views over the bay breathtaking. It was too late to do anything about it, for Ramón saw them and Joanna, catching his eye unwillingly, had perforce to go forward.

He was on his feet in an instant, pulling out his chair for Joanna to sit down and signalling to a waiter to bring two more chairs.

'Juana, Laurence,' he said smoothly. Ramón always kept his cool, Joanna observed. 'What a pleasant surprise. Do sit down.'

Two more chairs were put at their disposal by a waiter and Ramón ordered drinks, an iced beer for Laurence and iced lemonade for Joanna.

Candida was sipping her drink daintily. Her blue eyes were curious.

'Ramón,' she said sweetly, 'did you say Juana?'

'I did,' he admitted. 'It is Spanish.'

'Do you always give your English friends Spanish names?' Candida's blue eyes rested upon the drinks the waiter had bought on a tray and her fine eyebrows shot up at the iced lemonade he placed before Joanna. She took another sip of her gin and tonic, then said carefully, 'Is that why you ordered her lemonade?'

Joanna's fingers closed around her ice cold glass and lifted the sparkling drink to her lips. 'Ramón knows I like lemonade, Candida. I never drink alcohol other than wine. Cheers,' she said.

Ramón had taken a chair between Candida and Joanna. Casually he leaned sideways in his chair and, picking up the cheap sombrero Joanna had dropped beside her, handed it contemptuously to a passing waiter to dispose of.

'You came by car?' he asked politely.

Joanna nodded, feeling as out of place as the poor sombrero. Against Candida's sophisticated coolness, her own skin felt sticky with the heat and acting the fool most of the time with Laurence. Her feet ached with walking the hot streets and she longed for a cool bath. Laurence, catching her rather serious expression, smiled and winked. He had taken off his sombrero on entering the club and it now lay beside his chair. Joanna knew that he was thinking that Ramón was a bit stuffy. He was not really. To Ramón, she was someone special, a very dear friend and he was very protective to his women friends. Also, he hated anything cheap or tawdry.

Candida had seen his reaction to the sombrero when he had handed it to the waiter, but she made no comment. The incident was glossed over by Ramón ordering more drinks. As the waiter hurried away to do his bidding, he smiled at Joanna.

He said, 'I was telling Candida just before you arrived that my yacht, *El Gavilán*, has been in dock for repair and is due to arrive in Tenerife in an hour or so. As I have to go to Tenerife on business this weekend, it occurred to me that you could all accompany me on the yacht and see the sights.' He turned to Laurence. 'What do you say, Laurence?'

Laurence grinned. 'Sounds interesting. I appreciate your kindness. I'd be delighted, and thanks.'

Candida was clearly delighted. 'I've longed to go there since seeing it from the Villa Rosario. You mean we're to spend the weekend there?'

Ramón favoured Joanna with a mocking smile before giving his attention to the delighted Candida. 'We can use the yacht as a hotel, unless you would prefer to sleep ashore in a hotel. I assure you there are many splendid ones at your disposal.'

'Oh, I would prefer the yacht. It's a volcanic island, isn't it?' Candida leaned forward towards Ramón, her charming head on one side as she looked up into his dark face.

He smiled down at her. 'The peak of Teide, whose snow-capped summit you can see from the Villa Rosario, is surrounded by a volcanic crater. It is a giant of twelve thousand and two hundred odd feet and dominates the Canary Islands archipelago. The climate is perpetual spring, the scenery magnificent, picturesque towns and villages set among a flora of exotic flowers with the colourful costumes and folklore of the friendly inhabitants. There are not many beaches on Tenerife. But there are many hotels with swimming pools and a public lido.'

'Sounds heavenly,' Candida murmured. Joanna said nothing. She had been on Ramón's yacht many times with her father. It was fitted luxuriously and Ramón was the perfect host, but she had no desire to see Candida making a play for him. She felt a twinge of guilt on meeting Ramón's eyes as though she was betraying him in some way. Yet no man was more able to take care of himself. Besides, he might already be in love with Candida. His dark eyes strayed often enough to the golden hair, to linger on the blue eyes.

'You are coming also, Juana,' Ramón said softly, and smiled down at her warmly.

Her answering smile was a little bleak. It was the best she could do and he would, no doubt, think it odd. They had been such friends, and now this awful shutter seemed to keep dropping between them. The funny thing was Joanna was sure it was not all on her side. It was on the tip of her tongue to say, 'Are you sure you wouldn't prefer Candida to go with you on her own?' Then she told herself not be an ass and said, almost brightly,

'Yes, please. I saw a gorgeous paperweight in volcanic stone which I vowed to buy for Daddy the next time I was over. I hadn't enough money at the time. It was a lovely piece and had been polished.' She gave a small rueful laugh. 'If it hasn't gone, of course.'

Ramón said somewhat impatiently, 'Why did you not

come to me for the money? I would have bought it for you. You could have repaid me later if you wished.'

'I might have done had it not cost much, but I wasn't sure that I could ever afford it.' She spread expressive hands. 'After all, it wouldn't have been the same with someone else buying it for me.' Her smile was one of sunny appeasement. 'However, all is well. I sold a small painting the other day to an American tourist. Or rather,' a dimple appeared in her cheek, 'he helped himself to it from my easel and left a cheque.'

Ramón frowned heavily. 'I would not have counted the cost of any thing you wished to buy for your father. When did this incident with the American happen? Were you alone in the hills at the time?' He looked positively fierce.

'I went to one of the caves to take some fruit for a friend of mine who was ill. I wasn't away five minutes,' Joanna replied with some of the astonishment she must have felt at the time. 'The painting had gone and there was the cheque. The small Pepe, my friend's son, told me he had seen an American at my easel while I had been away.'

Ramón shrugged with distaste. 'I do not approve of you roaming the hills like you do. It is not becoming to a young woman. I shall speak to your father about it. He allows you far too much freedom.'

Candida cut in a little tartly, 'Why the fuss? Joanna needs the scenery for her paintings which she does marvellously. She has done one of me.'

'Indeed?' Ramón looked very interested. 'I would very much like to see this painting.' Again the dark eyes appeared to be entangled in the golden hair and blue eyes.

Joanna cleared her throat. 'I did it very quickly. It ... it was what I would call a tourist picture. But ... well, Candida liked it, so I gave it to her. And Ramón'—Joanna paused and looked at him appealingly—'don't say anything to Daddy about me going out into the hills. I'm a big girl now and there's nothing to make a fuss about.'

Ramón tore his eyes away from the golden hair and said with dignity,

'That is the crux of the whole matter, my dear Juana.

You are not a child any more. You would do well to remember that.'

And for once Joanna had no answer. For once in his deep smooth tones she seemed to sense a vague warning. What was he getting at, or who? Laurence?

The next day was another dazzling one and, when Joanna rose early and left her room clad in swimming gear, she was delighted to meet Laurence coming from his room wearing a beach robe over trunks and carrying a beach towel. His grin mirrored his own delight and when they went through the grounds to make their way to the garage for her car, Joanna discovered that they were holding hands.

After that most of Joanna's time was taken up with Laurence. They went swimming together in the early morning and riding in the hills in the afternoon. Laurence borrowed Nick's pony and Joanna took him to all her favourite haunts. In the evenings they went dancing and life became full to overflowing for Joanna, who hitherto had only her paints and her pony for company during the daylight hours when her father was in his study writing.

If Joanna's days were full, she was not the only one. Candida's were too. She grew more beautiful each day until she was positively blooming. On the few occasions that Joanna had met her with Ramón, he seemed unable to take his eyes off her, and no wonder. She was just like a film star going through her scenes and holding court, changing her clothes endlessly. For the rehearsals in the morning, she wore a trouser suit in pastel blue silk, changing for lunch into something in cool tailored linen. When Ramón came to pick her up in the afternoon she would flit out in a cocktail dress or something demure to gain his approval. And in the evening her dress overshadowed the lot. It was something so utterly feminine that Joanna wondered with mixed feelings how anyone could resist such a vision crowned with all that glorious golden hair. Certainly no man, and Ramón was very much a man. And Candida was terribly short of time. There was not a moment to lose.

Nick's play was to go on in London in the autumn and

rehearsals were well under way for the two leads. Part of the last chapter remained to be written, but Joanna knew her father could finish it in the wink of an eye once he had settled on it. Towards the end of the week, she went down to dinner early one evening to find him sitting on the verandah with a drink at his elbow. Laurence had taken Candida into Las Palmas for the afternoon to do some shopping, and Joanna had stayed at home to wash her hair and do a few neglected chores.

She sat on the arm of his chair and kissed her father's cheek. He looked at her fondly. 'You grow prettier every day. I like you in that headband around your hair. Your colour is changing. You're almost a blonde.'

She put a hand around the back of her head and lifted up the still damp heavy mass of hair. 'There's too much of it and it takes such a lot of drying. I'm tempted to have it cut off.'

He caught a handful of it and sniffed in the fragrance. 'It's beautiful. Don't you dare to have it cut. In my young days a woman's hair was her crowning glory.' He gave it a playful tug. 'You won't be my Joanna any more without it.'

She laughed and put an arm around his shoulders. 'Isn't it amazing how Candida and Laurence have fitted in here? It's going to be very quiet when they leave.'

He said, 'Would you like to go back with them to London for a while? I have friends there who'll be delighted to have you for as long as you want to stay. I haven't been very fair to you, have I? You've been cooped up here when you should be having a good time.'

Joanna had a sudden vision of a big city filled with excitement and moving masses, hunt balls, fashion shows, theatres, regattas and big fair Englishmen like Laurence.

'Daddy,' she said thoughtfully, 'wouldn't you like to go too? Think how nice it would be for you to attend the first night of your new play. After all, you do owe it to your public to show yourself.'

He took her hand. 'If I went it would be just to fly there and back again. It's so wonderful to work here all the time away from all the pressures and the noises not to mention the petrol fumes. Besides, the play doesn't go on until the autumn and it can be very cold in London.'

'Would you mind if I went?'

'Of course I wouldn't, only I would rather you went in the spring instead of the autumn.'

Her voice lightened as her fingers curled around his. 'You mean that?'

'Why not? I only hope you won't catch any chills. You'll need warm clothing. I don't want you to catch pneumonia.'

'Daddy, you know I'm never ill. You're a pet.' She bent down and kissed him.

Candida and Laurence came in at the last minute and had to hurry to wash and change for dinner. They were loaded with parcels which, Joanna guessed, were mostly Candida's. She appeared to be spending rather freely for an unknown actress. Furthermore, she had the look of someone who had come into money, Joanna thought. After dinner that evening Nick asked Laurence to join him in a game of chess and Candida took Joanna to her room to show her what she had bought that afternoon.

'This is for you,' she said, giving her a small parcel.

Joanna took it in surprise. 'For me? Why?'

'Because you've been so nice to me.'

Joanna blushed. 'Have I?' she said, still on a note of surprise as she stared stupidly at the parcel.

'Well, aren't you going to open it?'

'Sorry.' A pleasing delicate scent came from the package as Joanna unwrapped it to reveal a gold mesh evening bag. 'It's beautiful,' she cried, holding it up by the chain handle. 'It looks awfully expensive. Sure you can afford it?'

'Of course I can. I've something else for you too.' Candida went to the dressing table and picked up a cheque. 'This is yours. I sold your picture to Ramón. I'm giving you half the proceeds.'

Joanna made no attempt to take the cheque. 'I don't understand,' she said. 'What picture?'

'The one you did of me. When he saw it he wanted to buy it for himself.' She shrugged. 'I told him that I would give it to him for nothing, but he insisted upon paying for it—said he wouldn't feel as if it belonged to him if he didn't pay for it. So I humoured him. Anyway, it was very encouraging. He was quite taken up with it.'

'I see,' said Joanna, wishing she did see the reason for Ramón buying it. 'I don't want the cheque. I did give you the picture, and if you chose to sell it then it's your gain.'

Candida studied her for a moment with that familiar wry smile touching her lovely mouth. 'Suit yourself,' she said at last on another shrug. 'I'm not saying that the extra money won't come in useful, but I'd much rather you had a share of it. Sure you won't?' She held out the cheque coaxingly. 'You're not angry with me for selling the picture to Ramón, are you, Joanna?'

Joanna shook her head. 'Why should I be? It was your property to dispose of as you wished. Did Ramón say why he was buying it?'

Candida went to put the cheque down on the dressing table again. 'No, although the reason was obvious to me.' She turned round slowly. The small crooked smile still on her lips irritated as she said cheerfully, 'He wanted the picture because it was of me. We've been together quite a lot these last few days, or haven't you noticed?'

Joanna looked down unseeingly at the gold mesh evening bag, then looked up sharply when Candida, laughing joyously, crossed the room to hug her triumphantly. 'It's all thanks to you, my dear,' she exclaimed. 'That picture is going to remind him of me when I'm not there. And now I'll show you what I've bought for our weekend at Tenerife.'

She hummed a gay tune to herself as if the situation had been resolved to her own satisfaction and began to unwrap her parcels.

Nick did not accompany them on the jaunt to Tenerife. He was too busy with his play, but he drove them to Las Palmas in his big car, luggage and all. As they arrived on the quay Ramón's yacht greeted them like a huge graceful white swan on the water. Her name, *El Gavilán*, was painted boldly on her side, and a magnificent carving of a hawk graced her prow.

Supplies were being carried aboard and one of the crew came down the gangway for their cases. He was followed by Ramón, looking strong and vital in immaculate white slacks and a navy blazer with the family crest on the breast pocket. His hair gleamed darkly with the faint reddish tint in the strong sunlight and a white silk scarf worn elegantly around his firm brown throat gave a bronze glow to his skin as he strode towards them with a loose-limbed grace.

Joanna's heart gave a painful lurch at the flash of his charming smile and the way his eyes lingered eagerly on Candida. She was in blue this morning with white accessories. The wide-brimmed hat in white straw lent mysterious depths to her blue eyes as he bent his head over her white-gloved hand.

Joanna was in green linen with her brown hair a shining mass of glints from the sun. She was unadorned and looked as youthful and pliant as a young sapling.

Ramón bent his dark head over her hand with mocking eyes. 'Juana, you are as refreshing as a spring morning,' he teased. Then he was greeting Laurence and Nick. 'Welcome aboard *El Gavelán*.' His smile was replaced by a frown as Nick explained that pressure of work would prevent him from accompanying them. 'But you will come aboard for a drink to wish us bon voyage, Nick,' he demanded, putting an arm around his shoulders. 'There will be other times.'

While the crew took their luggage to their respective cabins, everyone gathered in the main *salón* for a drink. Ramón poured them out and passed them around, and Joanna accepted hers with mixed feelings. She had an uneasy feeling that her life was changing. Until now it seemed she had only been half alive with little or no knowledge of the world around her. In a way her life, until now, had been a closed flower which had never really opened. Life on the island had that quality, she supposed, and it was not a bad thing being only half aware of what was going on . . . if the increasing consciousness of it was going to prove unsettling. One could be plucked ruthlessly from one's own environment, and when that happened there would be no going back.

Her growing fondness for Laurence was exciting, but it was all mixed up with the feelings she had for Ramón. Ah well, maybe time would sort it all out. Later in her cabin, she took a shower and changed into a sun dress in glazed cotton with a bold pattern of brown and orange sunflowers on a white ground and trod into white open sandals. Then she brushed her hair and put on a matching band around her head for going ashore later when they reached Tenerife.

Candida joined her in the thickly carpeted corridor, looking ravishing in white with a matching white turban around her head.

'Isn't this fun?' she said, thrusting an arm companionably through Joanna's. 'I'm looking forward to going to Tenerife.'

Ramón and Laurence were already in the dining *salón* when they entered and a white-jacketed waiter was there pouring drinks. It was cool and pleasant with a slight breeze tempering the heat of the day as they sailed across the sparkling water, and the siesta afterwards on deck was a relaxing period before they reached Tenerife.

Joanna had visited Tenerife many times and she much preferred her own island, which was more lush and not so volcanic. It was a little after four when they sailed into the picturesque harbour of Santa Cruz between cruise liners and yachts beneath a hot shimmering sky. Camellias, roses, hydrangeas and oleanders filled the landscape with a riot of colour. People were bathing in the warm sea and sunning themselves on beaches and rocks. Many of them came from the Spanish mainland to enjoy the the intriguing solitude of the small numerous rocky bays outnumbering the beaches. In contrast to Las Palmas, the town of Santa Cruz clusters around the harbour, and provides the best centre for shopping.

The shop where Joanna had seen the paperweight she wanted for her father was in the rather narrow Calle del Castillo, the main shopping street of Santa Cruz. The shop was a handicrafts store dealing in handicrafts of bamboo and wicker work among other things. The stone she had fancied on a previous visit had obviously been sold, but a few words aside by Ramón to the proprietor brought nods and comprehending smiles to the man's pleasant round face. He went quickly to a room behind the shop and returned almost immediately with the paperweight she had admired.

The shopkeeper held the stone up to the light and the colours flashing from it were dazzling. 'Is it not wonderful, señorita? You admired it so much when you were here before that I saved it for you.'

Joanna gazed on the stone with enchantment. 'You did?' she exclaimed. '*Gracias, señor*. How much did you say it was?' She bent her head to look into her purse and missed the meeting of dark eyes above her head. Something flashed from Ramón's and the shopkeeper gave a barely perceptible nod.

When he named the price, Joanna gasped in surprise. 'You have reduced it? I'm sure it was more than that,' she said a little breathlessly.

The man's shrug was very Spanish. 'For you a very special price because you saw the beauty of it. Also it was, you told me, for your *padre*. So it is very special, is it not?'

Joanna laughed and gave him the money and he went to wrap up the stone. Candida and Laurence were looking at some rather nice baskets and wicker work at the other end of the store. Ramón's arrogant gaze was directed on her own enchanting face, a smile hovered around the firm mouth.

'So you have your stone,' he said. His look now was purely speculative. 'What I like most about you, my Juana, is your spontaneous warm response to small things. You are so eager, so refreshingly honest that you make me feel jaded.'

She shone up at him, excited and pleased at her luck in being able to purchase the stone she had saved for. 'I suppose you think me very naïve,' she said almost apologetically.

For a moment there was a strange gleam in his eyes. It was gone in a flash and he said seriously, 'You and I are old friends. There is something between us that is rather special. I am sure ...' he broke off abruptly as the shop-keeper approached with a small parcel neatly wrapped which he gave to Joanna. Then Candida was there to show them her purchases.

After that they were paired off in twos. Candida took charge of Ramón, leaving Laurence with Joanna. For the rest of the afternoon they went shopping and returned to the yacht in need of a bath and change.

That evening they all dined out at the most elegant resort on the island, Puerto de la Cruz, about twenty miles from Santa Cruz. Ramón had brought his car on the yacht and they motored there. During their meal they were serenaded by a Latin with a guitar and, later, they watched flamenco dancers under the stars. It was an enjoyable though curious evening for Joanna, who had experienced it all before. She sat in the back of the car on their return journey to the yacht and it seemed perfectly natural for her to put her head on Laurence's broad chest. It also seemed perfectly natural for him to slide an arm around her, hold her rather tightly and lower his head against hers. But she was unprepared for his next move to cup her chin with his hand and tilt her face to his. The kiss was gentle and Joanna had to admit she enjoyed it. It certainly set her pondering when she retired to her cabin later.

The following morning Ramón had to go ashore on business. It had been arranged for them all to go sightseeing on Santa Cruz when he returned. After Ramón had gone Laurence went to take a look at the engine room and both girls lounged on deck. Candida, looking beautifully cool and soignée in a primrose sun-suit, displayed lovely limbs on a lounger. Jonna, looking equally chic in a blue and white gingham dress, lounged beside her with a book.

Candida lifted a shapely arm and smoothed oil over it. 'You were very quiet in the back of the car last night with Laurence,' she mused. 'Were you indulging in a little petting?'

Joanna felt her face go a warm pink. 'Would you mind if we had?' she asked, lowering her book.

Candida laughed and went on applying oil. 'Gracious, no! Do you prefer Englishmen to Latins?'

Joanna closed her book. 'I haven't met many Englishmen, so I'm not at all sure. What about you?'

Candida shrugged. 'I've had a surfeit of Englishmen. I like your Marqués. In fact I like the whole set-up here.'

Joanna thought of Ramón and said evenly, 'Everyone likes the Marqués. But we live a different kind of life here. A gregarious type of person could find life somewhat restricted after a bustling place like London.'

Candida replaced the stopper on the oil, put it down beside her lounger and stretched out in an oddly sensuous gesture. 'I'm happy enough. I could stay happy here. In fact I can think of nothing more thrilling than being married here.'

'To . . . Ramón?'

'Who else? I'm different from his girl-friends here on the islands, and you must admit that golden hair and blue eyes are a change from dark lustrous ones and black hair.' Her brilliant smile met Joanna's thoughtful gaze. 'Of course, he's far too experienced to rush his fences. I don't suppose he'll propose without giving it a lot of thought. But I can wait.'

Joanna stirred and felt an impending headache, something she rarely had. Was it a sudden tenseness? An anxiety, a premonition, or was it a resentment of Candida acting like a cuckoo in her own little nest? Was she jealous of golden hair and blue eyes? Candida had closed her eyes and was already dreaming of life with Ramón on the island. Joanna looked at her watch and decided to go to her cabin to rinse her hot forehead in cool water. Ramón would be back any moment now to take them ashore.

However, she did not go to her cabin right away. Instead she walked around the deck to the shaded side facing the sea and leaned on the taffrail to look down on the water and enjoy the coolness on her face. As she closed her eyes all the tension pulling tightly across her forehead seemed to go. Footsteps sounded on the deck; she straightened, turned her head and her eyes collided with Ramón's as he strode towards her in his debonair fashion looking mocking and narrow-eyed in the strong sunlight.

His glance roved over her hair and rather pale face. 'All alone?' he queried. 'Where are the others?'

'Laurence was down the engine room and Candida is on deck. We're awaiting your return.'

He moved nearer to peer into her face. 'You look peaky. Too much sun or a bad head?'

Joanna forced a laugh, a small one. 'You're as bad as Daddy! I'm quite all right.'

Ramón paused, seemed about to say something . . . then it had passed. He slipped a monogrammed case from his pocket, selected a cheroot and lighted it with a matching lighter. Then he leaned his forearms on the taffrail beside her.

'Nick tells me that you are going to London when your guests return there. Are you worried at leaving your father?'

Joanna followed his gaze and looked across the sparkling water. 'No. It's a wonderful opportunity to do something I've always wanted to do, to see how other people live.'

'I agree. Why were you looking so sad just now? You should be wildly excited.' He blew out a thin line of smoke from his cheroot across the water. His dark eyes narrowed thoughtfully. 'You are not excited at the thought?' He turned his head and willed her to meet his questioning gaze.

She smiled. 'I am excited,' she insisted.

'Also a little apprehensive?' His eyebrows lifted ironically. He said softly, 'You have that frightened feeling which can appear sometimes in a dream when the sleeper knows it to be a dream and dreads the awakening. It will come, that complete break with your life here. I wonder what the experience will do to you?'

Joanna thought she detected a note of sadness in his voice. 'Nothing, I hope.' She laughed at the sudden tension between them, a breathless little laugh that was meant to be teasing. Somehow she was losing that quality of teasing Ramón, and he seemed to be losing it too. Things were not the same between them. She stood very still. A beautiful day. At this moment, perhaps, Candida and Laurence were preparing for their visit ashore. Candida would sit beside

Ramón in the front of the car and she would sit with Laurence behind them. Joanna felt something pinch at her heart. She said uncertainly,

'Why should you think I shall change?'

He gave her a smile that left his eyes enigmatic. His voice was cool. It placed a barrier between them. 'You will change,' he said inexorably. 'It will be a part of your growing up. Already you are unsettled since Laurence came. You like him?'

'Of course I do. I like Candida too, don't you?' she said steadily.

His eyes were almost black, black and glittering. 'That was not what I meant, but no matter.' He waved a brown expressive hand and she caught the glint of the ring on his little finger. 'I agree with your father that it is right for you to go to England. I know you will enjoy it. I might be going to London myself when Nick puts on his play.'

'You will?' Joanna was beaming up at him. 'I shall look forward to seeing you there.'

He said with whimsical inflection, 'We shall see. A lot can have happened to you by then. Meanwhile shall we enjoy our day? I think first we will visit El Teide. We must show our visitors our highest mountain. Come.'

The warmth of his charming smile focussed tenderly upon her brought an answering smile to her lips. 'Why not?' she answered.

They had an early lunch and set off in Ramón's car for the summit of the mountain. On leaving the harbour, he swung the car on to a road leading higher and higher through pine and eucalyptus forests. Far below were breathtaking views of palm-filled valleys and banana groves with the sea glistening under a cloudless blue sky beyond the island's curving shore. Gradually the lush greenness was left behind and they were confronted with a scene of bizarre beauty. Grotesque shapes of volcanic rocks in red, pink, yellow and black stretched as far as the eye could see and way down below Ramón's yacht was a toy in the harbour.

Ramón stopped the car in the shadow of the mountain and they all got out. Ahead of them was a cable car to take them practically to the twelve thousand and odd-foot summit. The journey was well worth it as a panoramic view opened at their feet of sea, islands and mountains in a blue haze of heat. Later, they sipped a glass of wine in a tiny bar near to the mountain's great crater, then made their way back to the cable car on the beginning of their downward journey.

CHAPTER FOUR

THE golden days passed and the arrangement of everyone going through the script of the play until lunch still stood. Candida still spent most of her day after lunch with Ramón, who entertained them frequently at Las Jacarandas in the evenings. Candida and Laurence were accepted by his friends with a studied politeness to which the language barrier contributed. As for Joanna, she was becoming more affected by Laurence as a man, finding a mounting excitement in his company.

With Ramón she had always been conscious of being a woman. With Laurence she was a companion, an equal person. But with Ramón always she had been that special gender, a woman, and for that reason important. The summer laid its carpet at her feet, unchanging in the golden brilliance of heat. Her relationship with the two men underwent no radical change. Ramón remained punctilious, holding her elbow sometimes, kissing her hand with that mocking twist of his firm mouth when they parted.

Laurence was content with leaving all the decisions to Joanna about where they spent their leisure. He smiled tolerantly at her warm friendliness and patent determination for him to enjoy every moment of his stay on the island. He was taken to places that she knew he would enjoy. As long as he found pleasure in her company, Joanna was satisfied. She asked no more of him than that he should find pleasure or gasp with surprise or be interested in everything she introduced to him, even to sampling new dishes or drinks.

Since that first kiss in Ramón's car his lips had not strayed further than her cheek. His reserve in this respect was due to her own behaviour. She shied away from him like a frightened colt whenever his arm happened to tighten around her and her partings from him at the end of each day were of very short duration, a peck on his tanned cheek no more.

One afternoon Joanna took him to her favourite beach. It belonged to Ramón and, being private, could be certain to be deserted. Rosita had packed a picnic tea for them and, after lunch, they went to her car where she stowed her beach bag and picnic tea in the boot along with Laurence's swimming gear.

From his seat beside her, Laurence grinned. 'Las Palmas gone sour on you?' he asked with the quirk of a brow as she headed for a different road.

'No. Just a secluded little spot where we can sunbathe. Actually, it belongs to Ramón.'

He admired her long bare sandalled legs, honey gold in their tan. 'Isn't that a bit risky?' he murmured.

'In what way?' Joanna blushed.

'Ramón and Candida might decide to go there also today,' he answered lazily, chuckling at the bloom of pink in her apricot cheeks.

'They won't.'

He raised a sandy brow. 'What makes you so sure?'

Joanna negotiated a tricky bend expertly. 'Ramón is Spanish and reserved,' she informed him gravely.

He chuckled again. 'I know what you mean. Is it true that it takes years for a man to get on speaking terms with his *novia*, and then only through her parents?'

Joanna nodded. 'Something like that. In Ramón's case, he has a position to keep up too. As he is a Marqués his choice of a bride will be much criticized by his relations, friends and employees.'

Laurence gave a quiet whistle. 'What do you think of his present leading lady, soon to be mine in the play?'

'Candida?' Joanna was deliberately evasive. 'You know her better than I do. So no comment.'

Her air of casualness was too calm to be real and Joanna gave her attention to the road, hoping Laurence would not notice. Right at this very moment Ramón could be driving along some romantic road with Candida beside him. And Candida, who had to pack everything in as much as she could from the moment of knowing Ramón, would not show any inhibitions. She was all out to grab her man.

'You're some girl, aren't you, Joanna?' Laurence drawled through her thoughts. 'Not in the least malicious or cynical.'

Joanna looked at him briefly through her lashes, smiled provocatively, and did it deliberately. She was acting completely out of character without knowing why. Perhaps a vision of Ramón and Candida in the intimacy of his car had roused little devils inside her. It was an attempt to provoke him into revealing just how much she meant to him. Or perhaps she wanted to make sure what her own feelings were towards Laurence. Was it just friendship, or was there more to it?

'As I've spent most of my days with my pony and paints I haven't had much practice in that direction,' she said. 'I might have some dark corners in my make-up which you know nothing about.'

He grinned with a flash of his usual good humour. 'I still say that you're some girl and one my mother would be delighted to see me with.'

'Thanks,' she said lightly, grateful to him for making a joke of it. Whatever had got into her to use the kind of coquettishness that she regarded as being so cheap in any woman? Really she ought to be ashamed. The sensible thing was to enjoy her day out just as Laurence was and avoid all complications. After all, they had not known each other five minutes.

The scenery was quite something to take her mind off problems; a series of shelves of caves clustered on the slopes leading down to the bay amid a lush growth of tropical plants and flowers. Carefully tended, they looked as though they had been there from the beginning of time. They parked the car in the foothills and, collecting their gear, made their way down to the beach. It was a winding path between overhanging bushes and greenery, half hidden. He followed her through cool green tunnels of honeysuckle and bougainvillaea, exclaiming with pleasure as each new archway opened up to a vista lovelier than the last. And he was gratifyingly impressed by the sudden appearance of the small secluded beach. A blaze of light came from the sea beyond.

'It's private enough,' Laurence agreed. 'Is this the only way to it?'

He squinted up at the cliffs as he spoke for another path, but saw none.

Joanna shook her head. 'I believe there is another way from Las Jacarandas. It's quite safe to swim here and we can dive out there at the far end from that shelf of rock.' She gestured to her far right at the end of the curve in the small bay where rock overhung the beach. 'There's also a cave there for you to undress. I'll undress here behind the greenery.'

Joanna took the picnic tea from him and put it on a shelf of rock under the cliffs, then went to undress. When she came into the warm sun in her swim suit Laurence was taking a perfect dive from the far end of the bay. He came swimming towards her in powerful easy strokes and she waded into the water and struck out. As she met up with him, they swam together and played in the water like two playful dolphins. She eluded him and he followed, chasing her out of the water and in and out of the rocks. They ended up again in the sea where they fought until they were breathless before lying panting on the warm sand. Then another swim and they walked up hand in hand to the shelter of the rock where Laurence spread out their beach towels and Joanna put out their picnic.

After opening the wine they popped olives into one another's mouths and washed them down. They ate the delicious food with relish, then put the remains back into the beach bag before stretching out side by side on the cool sand shadowed by overhanging cliffs. Out of the glare of the sun glittering on sea and sand Joanna, replete from food and drowsy from wine plus the exertion of swimming and fooling about, relaxed in the softly yielding sand and fell asleep.

Some time later, content and languorous, she awoke to find Laurence sleeping beside her. He lay with his hands clasped behind his head, breathing softly with a slight quirk to his mouth as though his dreams were pleasant ones. He looked so attractively boyish and nice in his teak tan that she bent over him to touch his cheek. His eyes opened immediately and stared up into her own. Then very gently he framed her face with his hands and drew it down as he shifted his gaze to her mouth.

It seemed to Joanna that one brief moment she resisted before giving him her lips. His kiss was gentle and the feel of his warm skin against her own was pleasant. But when he turned her over on her back, his kisses became more urgent. She responded at first, carried away with an eagerness that equalled his own as he whispered her name and punctuated each syllable with a kiss. Then her heart beating madly reached panic stations and she struggled to free herself. With a strength great enough to roll him over unawares, she was suddenly free and panting for breath. A strange desire that had been welling up inside her like an uncoiling snake shivered away, leaving her filled with a sick disgust. Moments ago, with his hands so urgent on her body, his breath on her face, Joanna had lost her own identity in a hunger of the flesh that hitherto had been alien to her.

Young and inexperienced though she was, she knew that promiscuous sex did not make for happiness. She needed to be loved not only for her body but for herself. It was fatally easy to mistake physical attraction for love, and her mind was not clear at the moment what she felt for Laurence. She had sprung to her feet, more upset by the fact that she had brought him to a secluded spot where they would not be disturbed than by the actual incident. Rigid with self-disgust, she raised her hands to her burning cheeks and looked down into his surprised face.

'What must you think of me—bringing you to this secluded spot? I—I didn't bring you here for—for what you think must be the obvious reason.' Her face felt on fire beneath her trembling hands. 'This place just happens to be one of my favourite spots. Please forgive me if I've given you a false impression. I didn't intend to flirt with you.' The thought of her provocative look in the car taunted her words. 'I—I am sorry. We are friends, aren't we?'

She looked down at him piteously. They stared at each other for several moments. Laurence's voice was of a controlled thickness when he answered. He shrugged.

'Look,' he said slowly, 'don't upset yourself. There's nothing to be sorry for. I know you well enough by now to put my own deductions on your behaviour now or at any time.' He gave a strained smile. 'It was as much my fault as yours. I got carried away. You're rather sweet, you know, and any man could lose his head over you quite easily. I didn't want this to happen, no more than you. At least, not yet.'

Joanna moved her hands to massage the tenseness in the back of her neck.

'I don't understand,' she said. 'What do you mean when you say, "not yet"?'

Laurence was sitting up on the warm sand supported by his hands acting as props behind him. He did not look at her as he spoke but stared out to sea his face rather pale beneath the tan. 'I think you know by now that I'm falling in love with you. You remember that I said that you were the kind of girl my mother would have approved of? Well, you're the kind any man, including myself, approves of too. When you leaned over me just now with that tender look in your eyes, I thought you were beginning to care for me in the way I wanted you to. I see now that I was wrong. I rushed you instead of giving you more time to get used to the idea of you and me.'

Joanna's fingers had moved once more to her scarlet cheeks. 'Oh dear, Laurence! I—I never thought for a moment—that—that you liked me so much. I would have behaved very differently had I known. It was natural for you to think what you did, especially since I brought you here to this secluded spot.' Joanna paused searching for the right words, not wanting to hurt him further. 'I like you too, but only as a friend. We are still friends, aren't we?'

She held out her hands to pull him to his feet, but he cast them aside roughly. 'Don't look at me like that,' he said harshly. 'Unless you want me to ravish you. Let's go.'

He rose to his feet and picked up his towel in silence. Joanna did the same, feeling utterly miserable. When she threw it over her arm and bent down to pick up her beach bag, Laurence was before her, swinging it up and grinning down at her, his humour partly restored.

'Don't look so shattered,' he teased, throwing a brotherly arm around her shoulders and kissing the top of her head. 'Is this your first experience with a man?'

She looked up in puzzlement at his twisted smile, trying to understand his sudden change of mood. If he had been hurt then he was hiding it very well. But he was an actor and had learned to create a mood at will.

Nevertheless he had been serious. He had not treated her as a chance for sex, someone to play with or just to make her feel good. And he was so very attractive, with the stray lock of fair hair straying on to his forehead. He must have had lots of affairs.

She said frankly, 'Yes. You must think me very naïve.'

His hands closed over hers as he gave her the beach bag. His eyes roved over her glowing face and clear eyes. 'I think you're wonderful, just like fresh spring water. We'll both forget what happened just now and go on from here.' He bent his head and kissed her hands. 'Agreed?'

Joanna nodded eagerly. 'Agreed. I want us to go on being friends. I like you very much, and you don't know what it means to me having you here. I might even fall in love with you, but I can't promise. You—you won't be very hurt if I don't?'

Joanna looked up at him anxiously. Laurence gave a philosophical shrug and suddenly he smiled, the same smile he seemed to reserve just for her.

'You worry too much,' he said. 'Let's see who can get dressed first.'

On the way back to the villa it was natural that their conversation was a little guarded and lacked spontaneity. A poor ending to what had promised to be a wonderful day, Joanna thought sadly. They both had to shed their awkwardness with each other or it would be awkward living under the same roof. Fortunately that evening Ramón was taking them all to the Spanish Club in Las Palmas for dinner. Nick was staying at home. He had writing to do, and Joanna felt like staying home too. She had to go, of course, to keep the number even, Ramón, Candida, Laurence and herself.

She began to dress for it without any real enthusiasm, knowing that Candida would be shrugging into another stunning dress. It was becoming a habit with her now to look at Candida's left hand each evening for a sparkling engagement ring—Ramón's. All too soon Ramón's car arrived. Candida was the first at the door, contriving to look ethereal and fragile in pale green floating draperies in spite of her height. Joanna followed, aware of Laurence and his look of appraisal at her slim white-clad sweetness. Ramón opened the door of his car, inclined his dark arrogant head above wide, white-clad shoulders and looked his usual dangerously attractive self. When the car swept away down the drive Joanna lay back against the expensive leather with Laurence beside her and tried to feel festive.

One would have to be completely out of sorts not to enjoy a night out at the Spanish Club, and Joanna was a young and healthy person with an appetite for good fare. Going anywhere with Ramón was always fun. He always managed to secure the best table and the maximum of service and courtesy. One quirk of a lean brown finger or an uplifted brow wrought miracles in efficient service. The meal and the floor show had been excellent, and now the band on a raised dais in one corner of the room was playing for dancing. Ramón was smoking one of his cheroots and Candida was dancing with Laurence.

Joanna sat staring down into her wine glass. Normally an evening out with Ramón was an event. Why then was she so restless? Why did everything seem common place and not exciting any more? Was it because of the proposed visit to England? It was, after all, a possible reaction. She had been unsettled since knowing she was going. And why not? She had looked forward to it for so long. That dream of shopping in the big London stores, going around the Tower of

London, the art galleries and museums would soon be a reality. She imagined herself at a glittering party with Candida and Laurence, being introduced to their arty and exciting friends. Then the thought arose that her father would miss her and he might even worry over her going thinking she might not wish to go back. After all, life in London would be vastly different from life on the island.

Perhaps she would regret going—at which thought she frowned down at slender fingers around the stem of her glass. It was a problem, especially as it had always been a dream at the back of her mind that she simply had to go to London. Not that she was not happy on the island, she was blissfully so. It was her father's fault really that she had this yearning. He had showered her with English literature and taught her that England was her heritage even though he did not intend to go back himself. Dear Daddy, Joanna thought tenderly. His excuse for not returning to England was mostly that the mild climate of the Canaries had softened him up too much to face the rigours of an English winter.

'Why so sad, Juana?'

Startled, she lifted a wide-eyed look to Ramón's dark intent gaze. He was watching her closely under those black lashes, his long flexible fingers curled around his cheroot. His eyes mocked the rush of colour to her face.

'I'm sorry, Ramón. I was deep in thought. Not actually sad but wrestling with a problem,' she admitted frankly.

He tapped the ash from his cheroot carefully into an ash tray fashioned from a colourful piece of volcanic rock.

'This problem seems to be of long duration. I have noticed this *tristeza* in you—an incomprehensible sadness—for some time. It is always a little bewildering for the young to be in love. However, do not despair. I happen to know that Candida has no designs upon Laurence. That is your immediate problem, is it not?'

He fixed his dark gaze on Joanna, who was discovering that she could not withstand it for long. She looked towards the dance floor at Candida and Laurence moving in synchronisation. 'No, it isn't that at all,' she babbled at once, then pulled herself up with a certain amount of comic dignity. 'You're wrong.'

Ramón lifted a tantalising brow, glanced negligently at the couple in question, then looked back at Joanna's flushed face. 'Am I indeed?' he said dryly.

'Yes. I'm sorry, Ramón,' she said placatingly. 'I'm being awfully rude in being so abstracted in your company. I must be a little tired after a rather hectic day out.'

'Tired?' echoed a derisive Ramón. 'Or unhappy? Why not tell me of the problem which causes the changing expressions across your face and makes you so tired?'

Joanna said as firmly as she could, 'It's a problem I have to solve myself. No one can help me because—well, it's been a dream for so long.'

'And now you are wondering if it can become a reality? Is it to do with Englishmen?' he probed.

Joanna's cheeks deepened in colour, leaving her momentarily speechless.

'In a way,' she temporised, looking cornered. 'There are some things one has to discover for oneself, for peace of mind.'

He raised a brow. 'True. Then why be so concerned about leaving your nest to fly away? You have had an excellent tuition and nothing can undermine your fundamental English upbringing.' He leaned forward. His dark eyes glittered and he said softly, 'It is too bad that you are afraid of love.'

Wild rose colour flooded her face and she cried indignantly, 'That isn't true! I've never been in love, not really in love.'

He shrugged expressively. 'One has only to look into your eyes to know that. Nick is very sensible to send you away.'

Joanna winced. 'You seem pleased at the thought.'

'You want to go, do you not?' he demanded.

'Of course I do.'

'Then there is the answer to your problem,' he retorted with a sardonic grin. 'The matter is settled. You will now begin to look happy.' Peremptorily he silenced further argument, and putting out his cheroot, rose to his feet. 'Come, let us dance.'

Most of the guests were dancing when Ramón took her into his arms and swept her away. Like most Latins he was an excellent dancer, but Joanna felt no joy in being his partner. She danced mechanically, although the band was playing a catchy tune which normally would make her feet tingle with rhythm.

'Still tired?' he inquired, after a few moments. 'You evidently had a hectic afternoon. Where did you go?'

'For a picnic,' she answered laconically.

'So,' he said dryly. 'You wore yourself out eating a picnic tea.'

Feeling a little irresponsible, Joanna admitted, 'We played about.'

'Indeed? Define "played about".' He sounded as cool as a glacier, and his fingers gripped hers tightly.

'We ran about the sand and had fun in the water.' She was aware of his sudden withdrawal, remembered that he was Spanish, and added almost apologetically, 'It was all completely innocent.' She wrinkled her nose at him in a gesture which swept away Spanish inhibitions in favour of English fun.

But Ramón was not looking at her. He was looking at a shining golden head not far away—Candida's.

The next few days were without any special incident. Joanna went into the hills on her pony each morning to set up her easel and paint. Then she returned home for lunch to join the rest of the household. And always there was the blue of the sea in contrast to white villas and exotic plants, and the deeper blue of the sky above. Joanna could make no legitimate complaint at not having enough to do. Every minute of her waking hours was completely occupied. Laurence monopolised her afternoons and evenings and she found it impossible not to grow fond of him. In a way he was rather like Candida, with the same impulsive generosity and real charm beneath a layer of sophistication which to

Joanna had seemed cold and impersonal on first acquaintance.

One morning she had done a portrait of Laurence after making a sketch of him. 'Like it?' she asked, showing it to him on arriving back at the villa.

'Very much,' he told her promptly, adding modestly, 'Am I really that good-looking?'

'Let me look.' Candida studied the painting over his shoulder. But her only remark was, 'Not bad. Don't give it to him. Make him pay for it. Some day, my love, you're going to be famous.' She looked up as Nick entered the room. 'Come and look what your gifted daughter is turning out now—portraits.'

Nick laughed. 'Have you gone to portraits, Joanna? This I must see.'

'Nothing special, Daddy. I mean, with apologies to the sitter, I'm just learning to get the hang of it.' Joanna laughed at Laurence, who was still studying his likeness.

'All the same,' Nick admitted after a keen perusal of the painting, 'I'd say you had a flair for it, my pet. Would you like to be a commercial artist?'

Joanna looked at him in horror. 'I'm not good enough.'

'You're too good for that kind of thing,' Laurence cut in firmly. 'At least I shall be certain to have a bit of fame in the future as one of the subjects for that celebrated artist Joanna Main.'

They all laughed at this and, as Rosita came to announce that lunch was ready, the sound of a car being driven up to the villa came to them through the open windows. It was Ramón. He was wearing a lightweight linen suit, silk shirt with a smart tie. He looked handsome and debonair, with twice the vitality of anyone present and infinitely more zest for life.

'What is this?' he asked politely. 'Another portrait. May I?' He picked up the portrait which Laurence had stood against the wall of the room and looked at it for some moments in silence. 'Undoubtedly well done,' was his comment. 'Nick, this daughter of yours has an exceptional talent. I suggest she has an exhibition of her paintings.'

Nick smiled. 'Not a bad idea. Shall we go in to lunch? I thought you weren't coming, Ramón. You're usually here for a drink before lunch.'

Ramón stood the portrait against the wall, straightened and gave his charming smile. 'Unfortunately, I was delayed,' he said.

He went on to explain the reason for his delay and Joanna walking behind him to the dining room felt the power of his presence. It was his intelligence, his sensitivity, his hard core of arrogance and integrity which drew her to him. There, under the disciplined man he had allowed himself to become, was the flame, and Joanna knew it. His wife would be very fortunate indeed. It was kind of him to keep insisting upon an exhibition for her work, but the thought terrified her. She told him so at lunch, seated beside him with Laurence on her other side. The subject had been brought up by Laurence, who teasingly asked her how much she wanted for his portrait.

'Take it with my love,' she told him simply.

'The fact is,' remarked Ramón, smiling tightly, 'you are an artist of considerable ability and we all recognise that your work may one day be worth a fortune.'

Joanna had no pretensions and refused to take her painting seriously. Suddenly she laughed. It was a nervous reaction to the mere idea of taking her work seriously.

'I'm sorry,' she said feeling everyone's glances upon her. 'You see, it's one thing to paint for the sheer joy of it and quite another to paint by order.' She shrugged slim shoulders to add weight to her argument. 'Besides, who's to know that the talent, if any, only exists while I'm on the island? I could lose it when I go to England.'

Ramón said darkly, 'One may lose much when going to another country, but not, I think, a talented gift.'

Joanna sought her father's help, looking across the dining table at him with eloquent gaze. He gave a sardonic grin and winked at her.

'Ramón is right, my pet. Talent seems to run in the family and as such cannot be entirely lost in different surroundings. I imagine that Ramón is latching on to this gift of yours as something to concentrate on to keep you occupied in your adolescent years. Like me, he still regards you as a child.' He lifted a hand as she was about to protest. 'In some ways you're a complete baby, in others so very wise for your age, thanks to my efforts at being both parents rolled into one.'

Joanna lifted a determined chin, quelling rising anger against the two men who meant so much to her, her father and Ramón. 'Daddy,' she said forcefully, 'I shall go to England to have fun with a capital letter. Furthermore, I am not going to paint by order. One famous person in the family is enough.'

'You'll certainly have fun,' put in Laurence lazily. 'You'll have more dates than you can cope with.'

Candida said nothing being content with remaining silent, although her eyes resting on Ramón were very alert. It was he who had the last word.

He said with a hint of satire, 'Talent will out. Go to England, Juana. There you will see much that you want to paint, and I warrant your paintbrushes will not be idle for long.'

His dark eyes held a satirical look and Joanna was irritated at what, to her, was his indifference to her going. She had no idea that he had been invited to lunch. Not that it mattered only these days she liked to be prepared for his coming. Of late it had been his intent look that she was finding it hard to withstand. Now it was becoming his presence as well. He was taking Candida out that afternoon after lunch and Joanna was going to her room to change when he stopped her. Laurence had already gone to his room and Nick to his study, so they were alone in the hall. There was a hint of auburn in the raven black hair caught in the sun's rays slanting across the room from the window. His face was a bronze sculpture, a very handsome one. Joanna felt a subtle perceptiveness clear in his friendship towards her and the quiet twinkle in his eyes did not escape her.

He said softly, 'You spoke at lunch about not wanting to paint to order. Am I to understand that you are serious about this?' There was a disturbing insistence in his eyes as they flicked over her changing expression. 'If so it seems that I am too late with my request. Are your friends included in this refusal to paint for profit?'

At first Joanna could only stare and take in his unexpected remarks. Then her affection for him plus his disturbing presence pushed aside the tensions and questionings that filled her mind and she smiled up at him brightly.

Her voice was openly teasing. 'Don't tell me that you want me to paint a picture of yourself, Ramón?'

His smile was wholly charming. 'I want you to paint a portrait of Abuela. She has many portraits of herself when young, but none since she has grown older. You will do this for me, *pequeña?*'

His voice lingered caressingly on the last word, a fact which completely escaped Joanna, who was staring at him in surprise.

'You want me to do a portrait of your grandmother? The Marquesa?' she gasped.

His mouth quirked in amusement. 'You do not approve of Abuela having her portrait painted? I can asure you that she will be delighted if you do her the honour of asking her to sit for you. You made a magnificent job of Las Jacarandas.'

Joanna gave a pained smile. 'Ramón,' she remonstrated, spreading out her hands and looking at him despairingly, 'it's one thing to paint a view and quite another to paint a portrait. I'm not a gifted artist. Painting just happens to be my hobby. I just daydream on canvas, that's all.'

'Then you daydream very well.' He looked at her quizzically. 'You are funny, *chica*, a mixture of youth, innocence and honesty combined with exceptional gifts which you are too modest to admit to.'

Joanna looked up at him wide-eyed. In the filtering sunlight from bougainvillaea-framed windows, the clear-cut arrogant features were very striking, his teeth very white against the smooth tan of his face. But this was no time to dwell on his undoubted charms. She was worried, her shrug was a nervous one.

'Anyone can paint if they give their mind to it. I've had nothing else to do. Daddy is writing most of the day and I filled in my leisure with a hobby, and that's all it is.'

Joanna bit her lip. How could she tell him of her loneliness through the years, the aching need for her mother? Rosita had done her best, but it had not been the same. Ramón was leaning elegantly against an archway in the hall. His look was a long slow one as he listened. It was one of his charms that he listened. He never contradicted what was obviously true, nor did he hasten to comfort, a comfort which in his case could be no more than a verbal one.

'True,' he agreed laconically. 'A hobby which disclosed a latent talent.'

She floundered beneath his intent regard. 'So you say,' she conceded. 'I—I don't know. I only know that I paint because I want to paint spontaneously from the heart. It's—it's something one can't do to order. Besides, I'm going to London soon. You heard what I said at lunch—that I mean to have a good time like, like other girls of my age—and that means no commitments.'

Ramón sighed. 'I had hoped——' He pulled himself together as if regretting the words and went on with some restraint. 'As far as I am concerned, and knowing how much you will desire it, the subject of the portrait is now closed.'

He gave a small polite bow and took a couple of strides across the hall, presumably on the way outdoors where he would wait by his car for Candida to join him when she was ready. Joanna stood where he left her, torn between running after him and going to her room to get ready for her afternoon with Laurence. She chose the first. The disappointment on his face had been too much. Flitting after him, she barred his way and looked up at him appealingly.

'I'm sorry, Ramón,' she said huskily. 'If it means so much to you I'll paint the portrait.'

He raised a dark silky brow, seemed unimpressed and spoke laconically.

'You will?'

She nodded eagerly. 'On one condition—no payment. It will be a gift.'

'No gift,' he announced, and calmly lifted her aside out of his path.

He had taken a couple of long strides across the hall when she confronted him again, barring his way.

'But don't you see?' she pleaded. 'It has to be a gift with no payment.'

He glowered darkly. 'No, I do not see. I requested the portrait.'

Again she was lifted from his path with consummate ease and placed gently aside. He had almost crossed the hall when she leapt in front of him again.

'All right,' she conceded, 'have it your own way. You will pay me one escudo, no more, no less.'

Ramón winced. He was very near, so near that her mind registered the tanned perfection of his face. It had deepened to a dull mahogany and left him momentarily speechless.

'One escudo?' he echoed in disgust, so fiercely that Joanna blinked.

'One escudo,' she repeated as firmly as she could, and added forcefully, 'If you're a gentleman, you will accept.'

He looked thoughtful. The black eyes glittered dangerously. Then he put on a slow sardonic smile. 'I shall take you to Abuela in the morning and bring you back in time for lunch.'

'But—but, Ramón——'

He dismissed further argument peremptorily. Arrogantly, he announced. 'The matter is settled,' and, lifting her out of his way as he spoke, he put her down to one side and made for the door. '*Adios, chica.*'

'Just like that,' Joanna informed the empty air, and headed thoughtfully for her room. He had not addressed her with his usual, 'My Juana.' The endearments had been there, but they were not the same as his favourite name for her. Could it be that he was already paving the way to announce his engagement to Candida, who had hurried to her room immediately after lunch to make herself beautiful for him? The thought was not a happy one, bringing with it the sense of loss which had never quite left her since the death of her mother. She had been too young at the time to feel a real sense of grief, but the sense of loss, of uncertainty, had remained.

Candida met her on the stairs, looking even more beautiful in a full-skirted dress of the palest yellow. A wide-brimmed cream straw hat matched the raffia embroidered bag and open-toed sandals. She was all sparkle and very feminine. Joanna's heart grew cold as she met the blue eyes, knowing that Candida's every action was for Ramón's benefit.

'Is Ramón indoors or is he waiting for me in his car?' Candida was asking. 'I know he hates to be kept waiting long.'

'Ramón has gone outdoors to his car,' she answered with a smile. 'Have a nice time.'

'Thanks. You too.' Candida drifted down towards the hall on a wave of exclusive perfume, leaving Joanna a little breathless as she went rapidly upstairs. As she reached her room she knew it was not the sudden ascent that had quickened her heartbeats. Caught unawares by the vision of Candida, her thoughts had veered once again to Ramón. What she felt for him was more, much more than affection. But was it love? Was this the reason that she would find it so easy to dislike Candida whom she now liked so much? A clock striking the hour in the hall below reminded her that Laurence would be waiting and she changed hastily, putting all disturbing thoughts behind her.

They took their ponies into the hills that afternoon and left them tied to trees while they explored the caves accessible only on foot. The ponies plucked at the grass contentedly as they left them to graze and move upwards with the gentle sounds of nature around them, a coaxing gentle voice herding goats in a far-away green spot, the gentle flutter of wings causing shadows on the ground from movement overhead. They fell into step together up the winding path.

Laurence was studying her quietly, the lovely line of her delicate profile, the swinging silky curtain of hair and the long slender, honey-gold limbs. 'Why are you so eager to go to London?' he asked quietly.

Joanna had been looking ahead with the dreamy gaze of the artist. Now she turned her head and her gaze was clear and direct, between lashes which cast shadows on the delicate contours of her face.

Frankly, she answered, 'I suppose I feel cheated of not knowing how the rest of the world lives. I'm young and I want to have fun.'

'You know a great many English girls who live in the provinces say that and they all go to London. But many of them find that they don't fit in.'

Her eyes were frankly curious. 'You mean the weight of tradition is too much for them?'

He laughed. 'Good heavens, no! Tradition has gone by the board crushed by the jackbooted giant of progress. No, many of them are disillusioned. They expect too much. Instead of dreams coming true they find stark reality.'

'Is that bad?' she asked.

He shrugged broad shoulders. 'Depends upon how you take it. I've been wondering how you will fit in. You seem to belong here like some delicate flower that needs sun, air and space in which to bloom.'

'Only because I've grown up here. Don't forget we're English. Daddy is as English as you. He stays on here because he finds the climate much kinder to what he calls his ageing limbs. Also it's a restful place for him to write. His difficulty will be ever to leave here. I don't know about me yet.'

She glanced at him and when he did not answer she searched his face. It struck her forcibly that he was handsome, if strongly cut features, a square jaw and well shaped head added up to it. And that straw-coloured hair was an added attraction. Strange that she and Ramón should both be interested in fair-haired people. And thinking of Ramón, compared with Laurence he was more than just handsome. His Latin looks had something definitely more rare, a certain sensitivity, a strength and wisdom which along with his charms made him unforgettable. They stepped aside for a laden donkey, its panniers bursting to capacity, coming up the hill. Laurence allowed his fingers to seek her hand and curl around it.

'Buenos dias, Francesca,' Joanna said to the buxom woman following behind.

Teeth flashed in the olive face. '*Buenos dias*, Joanna, *señor*.' Francesca's politeness was wholly Spanish, and she continued on her way.

They watched as she passed over a rise in the hill and out of sight.

'These people seem to love you, Joanna. What is this magic you possess which draws everyone to you?' Laurence turned towards her speculatively.

Joanna laughed. 'There is no magic. I've known these people from a child. Come, I'll show you where Francesca lives.' They began to walk up the incline together, swinging clasped hands as they went. 'Francesca lives in one of the caves in the hills. The cave-dwellers aren't primitive, you know. Their dwellings are spotlessly clean and hewn out of rock. Francesca has a kitchen and a bedroom and beautiful hanging plants around the entrance to her home.'

'Sounds like paradise with someone like you,' Laurence murmured as they topped the rise. His eyes were on the snowy peak of Tenerife. 'I can understand your father loving this place. The sensation of silence and space is terrific.' Immediately below the path meandered into two. The path to their left led to the caves rising starkly in the granite hills and on to the woods beyond. The other path sloped downwards to the valley and the banana groves among fields of maize.

Francesca had taken the path to the caves and, as they watched her reach her dwelling, the scarlet of her dress showed vividly against the whitewashed entrance. She presented a colourful picture with the little donkey standing there placidly beside her.

'Let's rest,' suggested Laurence suddenly, and pulled Joanna down on the sweet grass. The silence around them was deep and profound, broken only by the echo of a distant goat bell. Laurence lay on his back squinting up at Joanna, who sat beside him. From where he lay her loose shining hair glinted with golden streaks in the sun. Her thick lashes looked spiky and silky and her slim brown arms and slender neck had the soft bloom of a ripe peach.

Joanna was slightly embarrassed beneath his scrutiny, with an intense feeling that many things between herself and this attractive man watching her so closely would be better left unsaid. In the crystal clarity of the air and the enfolding warmth of the sun a sensation of exhilaration crept through her. Her heart was beating with a new primitive longing as Laurence smiled slowly up at her, thrusting her into a new world of conflicting emotions. Already she felt much older since knowing him. He did not speak, but she understood the message in his narrowed eyes as clearly as though he had drawn her into his arms and was kissing her. With a wisdom beyond her years, Joanna knew that passion could mislead, physical attraction could fade and that desire had to be more than a sudden appetite. It had to be true, strong and powerful, springing from the deep roots of true love. She was beginning to realize that there was nothing casual or halfhearted about it. Not for her. It had to be the real thing from the start.

More than ever now it seemed essential for her to go to London, if only to bring her life into some kind of perspective. The overwhelming masculinity of Laurence had taught her that, happy though she had been on the island, she could not continue as she was through the years.

'You look pensive and very beautiful,' Laurence was saying, taking her hand and closing his fingers around it. 'Something on your mind?'

The colour rushed up under her clear skin and she looked away from his intent gaze to see the white turrets of Las Jacarandas enclosed in greenery on a distant hill.

'Ramón wants me to do a portrait of his grandmother. He's taking me to see her tomorrow morning,' she answered.

Laurence raised a brow. 'Good for you! That should get you more orders.' He gazed for a long moment at their clasped hands and frowned. 'But didn't I hear you say that you weren't going in for that sort of thing?'

Joanna followed his eyes, and tried to pull her hand away from his grip. He seemed unaware of her intention, for he continued to clasp her hand closely. So she left it there.

'That's right, I did,' she admitted reluctantly. 'But Ramón was so disappointed when I refused, and hurt, that I felt in the wrong. So I agreed to do the portrait.'

'Even though you didn't want to do it? I call that a very kind act of yours. But it couldn't have been so important to a man like Ramón who can commission the finest painters in the land to do his family portraits?'

'I know.'

'Do you know this lady who's to sit for you?'

She nodded. 'The Marquesa is sweet and I would hate to hurt her. You see, Ramón could have discussed it with her before asking me. I should feel unkind if I refused now.'

He squeezed her hand. 'You couldn't be unkind to anyone—that's what I like about you, and the thought is very comforting.' He smiled at the puzzled look in her eyes. 'I'm thinking of when I propose to you,' he teased.

Again her colour deepened and a sudden warm feeling for him filled her.

'You really are sweet, Laurence. Tell me about your life in London and all about your flat there.'

He released her hand then and, supporting himself on an elbow, began to talk about himself.

CHAPTER FIVE

JOANNA dressed with more than her usual care the following morning for her visit to the Marquesa. She was rewarded by Ramón's obvious approval, for he stood for several moments looking at her white sleeveless dress and taking in the fondant blue wide-brimmed hat, matching gloves, bag and dainty sandals. Her make-up had been light, a merest touch of blue on her eyelids, a protective cream and a delightful touch of lipstick. Because the visit was rather special, she had used a subtle touch of perfume behind each ear.

If Ramón was pleased with her appearance she was equally delighted with his. In the strong morning light he looked virile and disturbingly handsome in a grey lightweight suit, maroon silk shirt and sober pale blue tie. The dark crisp hair sprang in tendrils where they had resisted the disciplined brushing and his dark eyes were keen and smiling.

She said shyly as he assisted her into the front seat of the large opulent car, 'I have my notebook with me to write down the colours I shall require. There will be no problem there, as I have a fresh stock of paints.'

Ramón nodded his approval and slipped into the seat beside her. The strong brown hands set the car in motion and they slid away. Candida and Laurence were already in Nick's study going through their lines. Joanna wondered what Candida would think of her new assignment, and it occurred to her on a note of surprise that she had never thought about it until now. In any case, Ramón had said they would be back for lunch.

He handled the car with his usual skill, taking the slope down at a decorous speed. He spoke little at first, sweeping around blind corners and putting on speed with smoothness and a relaxed precision. The villa of the Marquesa was on the outskirts of Las Palmas. One turned off the main highway to a road which led eventually into the shadow of the mountains. It was some time since Joanna had been there. The Marquesa led a quiet and secluded life and had been away staying with a relative for several months until recently, so Ramón was saying.

'The villa has been redecorated and all the panelling stripped and polished,' he stated. 'It is essential as one grows older that there should be no reminder of advancing age by the deterioration of one's surroundings.' He turned briefly to give her his charming smile. 'Abuela was very reluctant for it to be done, but now she is very happy about it and that her portrait by a modern young artist will go well with the new decor.'

'You have told the Marquesa of our impending visit?' Joanna asked in surprise.

'Of course.' The mobile mouth tilted. 'You could not possibly paint her portrait without her being aware of it.' He swung the car off the main highway to make for the range of mountains in the distance. 'It will be interesting to know what you think of the villa in its new dress,' he went on as the big car swallowed up the miles to bring the hills nearer.

Joanna looked out on the island scenery with her usual intense pleasure in it as the car left the flat land and began to climb. Soon they would see Las Palmas beyond the hills in a soft haze of heat edged by white-frothed blue waters of the bay. By that time they would have arrived at the Villa Faustino, the home of the Marquesa. It was an elegant place built by craftsman of long ago—gardens, courtyards, fountains and high-ceilinged rooms divided by Moorish arches, and the windows giving impressive panoramic views. Joanna imagined it would look fabulous in the new decor. What a dear Ramón was to think so much about his grandmother as to make sure that her surroundings did not become depressing. Not that such a fabulous dwelling could ever be described as such.

She voiced her thoughts as colour-washed houses and churches were seen up the hillsides looking like part of the landscape in their muted colours.

Dreamily, she said, 'I've always loved the Villa Faustino. When I first saw it years ago as a child, I imagined fairies in the lovely gardens.' She laughed, a soft laugh of pure pleasure, as she added, 'I'm sure I thought that they were in the grounds of Las Jacarandas too.'

Ramón turned to look at her with a slow smile. 'But of course there were,' he said, giving his attention once more to the road ahead. 'You were a fairy yourself. I am sure they are still there. It is important to me that you like my home. Abuela is, by your English standards, a little behind the times. But she is wise in her experience of life like many others of her age. We Spanish value our dignity, a dignity which is extended to the poorest in the land. I do not think it is a bad thing.'

She reviewed his incomparable profile tenderly. 'Neither do I, Ramón. There's a certain gallantry in the way you look after and protect your grandmother.' During the conversation the barrier between them lifted and they seemed to be on the old footing of happy camaraderie. She smiled a little wickedly. 'One wonders how you would treat a wife.'

Ramón kept his eyes on the road ahead as he negotiated a tricky bend. His reply was casual. 'We Spaniards are passionate people, so I do not think she would have cause to complain, especially if she were Spanish.' He cast her a swift glance and noted her hot cheeks. 'So,' he said softly, 'you have marriage in mind, *chiquirritica*. The blond Englishman has entered your dreams and you have forgotten the fairies.'

Joanna laughed slightly, irritated by his manner towards her. Defensively, she cried, 'I'm not a child any more! I'm grown up. Besides, I don't think it has much to do with Laurence. What about you and Candida? She's blonde too, and you're in her company a great deal.'

She glanced at him swiftly, hoping he was not annoyed with her for being so personal. That he had been personal with her did not occur to her. After all he was the Marqués de Orleron y Faustino, and no one, not even close friends, dared to question his way of life.

'So you think I also have marriage on the mind?'

Her colour deepened. 'Just wondering,' she replied demurely, and was surprised by the sudden heavy beating of her heart. Holding her breath, she waited for his answer.

'If I had married every woman I had been friendly with I should have had a harem by now. It is different with me. I am a man of experience and more years than yourself,' he admitted evenly.

'Candida is very beautiful,' she said.

'I had noticed,' he temporised, looking in no way cornered. There was a short silence. Finally, he said; 'Do you really think that a woman's beauty is sufficient to add up to a good marriage?'

Joanna hesitated. Then she blabbered, 'I ... I would say it ... helps ... to attract the person one is ... fond of.'

'And you would advise me to marry Candida?'

'Of course not!' she began indignantly, then stopped in an effort to control her look of dismay at the thought. 'I never said that.'

'No, you did not,' he agreed coolly. 'Neither did you say you were going to marry Laurence. Are you?'

She borrowed a little of his coolness. 'I'm not going to marry anyone yet,' she said quickly. 'You forget I'm going to London. I've wanted to go for years.' She drew a deep breath. 'I want to see everything that makes it the most exciting city in the world. I want to visit the Tower of London, the Tate Gallery, picnic on Hampstead Heath, watch the Changing of the Guard and stroll down the Portobello Road.' The words tumbled out until she wondered where they had all come from. Breathlessly she met his gaze, a dark intent look which somehow caught at her heart.

'I hope you have fun,' he said.

They did not speak again and Joanna sat as he drove on, feeling the warmth of their companionship shivering away, to be replaced by a slight nervousness. They were among well cultivated land and following a road edged by marvellous trees. When the car swerved slightly, she held on to the door as it slid into the cool green light of a delightful courtyard. It was spacious and overlooked by tall windows shuttered with freshly painted wooden slats and iron balustrades. A balustrated gallery ran around the first floor, festooned underneath with hanging plants of every hue. On the tiled courtyard surrounding a fountain were vines, trees and shrubs in earthenware jars. The rays of the sun gave it a strange fantastic beauty and the dramatic impact was even more than Joanna had remembered. When Ramón opened her door and helped her out, she said with pleasure, 'How lovely it is! I'd forgotten it was so fabulous.'

'Strange you should feel so, because it explains my own sentiments entirely,' he said, taking her elbow lightly in the way he had of always making her feel cherished, and leading her across the handsome tiled floor to the heavy oak door. 'To have such a place is delightful. It is still more delightful to also have an Abuela to visit.'

They had passed into a wide room of tall cool windows beautifully balanced. Chandeliers glistened like jewels from an ornate ceiling, Persian rugs covered a tiled floor and beautifully carved elegant furniture was offset by freshly decorated walls in a rich silk damask. The overall effect was one of muted wealth and good taste creating a perfect setting for gracious living and contentment.

Softly Ramón said, 'What do you think?'

Joanna's deep sigh was one of fervent admiration. She shone up at him and exclaimed, 'It's beautiful! Everything is so fresh, as if the old character of the place has been refreshed by a shower of spring water.'

'You do not think then that I should have modernised it?'

She shook her head. 'You could hardly do that. Your grandmother would not have felt the same in strange surroundings. Besides——' her delighted gaze took in the beauty of other rooms he led her through all richly furnished but nevertheless luxuriously comfortable and relaxing.

'Yes, *pequeña*?' he prompted softly, still holding her elbow in that warm protective grip.

Her attention came back to his dark intent gaze, finding it harder to withstand with every second. Her laugh was as refreshing as the spring water she had mentioned and she said teasingly, 'Besides, it's the Villa Faustino. It would cease to be so if it was modernised.'

'True,' he agreed laconically. 'And now we must drink to it.'

They were in the main *salón* and he waved her to a damask tub chair while he strode to an ornate sideboard containing a tray of wine glasses and a bottle.

'Only a little for me, please,' Joanna implored.

He laughed and strode forward with two glasses of golden liquid to hand her one. 'It will calm your nervousness,' he assured her. 'Abuela can be a little formidable to the young. She has little or no contact with the outside world only when she is out in the car. Sometimes it is better for the peace of mind of the elderly not to know too much.' A sardonic smile lifted the corners of his firm mouth, revealing strong white teeth. 'No doubt she will have her own opinion of the young people she sees on her rare visits to the cities, seeing in their casual dress the need to economize in their way of living. It would never occur to her that they now choose to live that way.'

They raised their glasses to each other and drank leisurely. Ramón explained about the renovation of the villa and admitted to considering putting Las Jacarandas through the same process. Joanna listened while he leaned elegantly against the Spanish fireplace, knowing that he was probably getting Las Jacarandas ready for his bride. There was nothing specific to go on even now in the matter of him and Candida. But in some way Ramón had changed. Since Candida had arrived that charming smile of his had become rare, his teasing manner was rare also, which could only mean one thing, that he was in love.

He could not know that Candida was a ripe plum ready to fall into his hand. Why else would he look so sad? Should she tell him? Joanna emptied her glass and perished the thought. He was quite capable of finding his own wife. Indeed, she was of the opinion that he would make love deliciously, with that arrogant charm that would melt one's limbs at his touch.

He took her glass, set it with his own on the tray on the sideboard and consulted his watch.

'Abuela will be about to have her mid-morning chocolate, so we will now go to her room,' he said.

As though on cue a middle-aged woman dressed severely in black appeared in the arched doorway. '*Buenos dias*, Señor Marqués, *señorita*,' she said in a soft voice filled with respect.

Ramón answered in cultured Spanish, asked a few questions crisply and turned to Joanna on receiving the softly spoken reply.

'Abuela is waiting for us,' he told her with a smile, and they followed the woman from the *salón*.

Concepta Maria, Marquesa de Orleron y Faustino sat awaiting them in her *salón* on the first floor. She looked very regal, sitting straight-backed in her chair with a rigidity of the spine which denoted an excellent carriage and disciplined grace inherited from Spanish nobility. Like Ramón's, her deportment was graceful, well-mannered and serene. The brilliant dark eyes rested tranquilly upon them in a courteous and delicately searching look as they entered the room. The gracious smile became one of reminiscence when her eyes passed over Joanna's slim form to rest on Ramón. She was probably seeing in him the beloved husband who had died several years ago.

He went forward to kiss her on both cheeks and murmur a greeting. Then Joanna went forward to kiss the cheek proffered. It was slightly scented of sandalwood soap and remarkably unlined—the Marquesa had never been one for sitting in the sun without a sunshade. Her hair was still of an ebony blackness and parted in the centre to form two glossy curtains of hair for her small face. Her face had a peach-like bloom and it was only when she smiled that the lines appeared. Mid-morning chocolate was served along with small almond pastries which melted deliciously in the mouth.

Joanna sat down in her chair, feet and slim legs together demurely and accepted her hot chocolate and a pastry. Ramón declined and went out of the *salón* to have a word with the workmen, who were still at the back of the villa.

The Marquesa watched him go with a sigh and put down her hot chocolate only half drunk. 'Ramón reminds me so much of his grandfather,' she confided in Spanish, dabbing her lips delicately with a wisp of lace. 'The same easy charm that swept me off my feet all those years ago. He was ten years older than I. I was about your age, Joanna, when we were married.'

Joanna had eaten her pastry and she smiled warmly. 'You must have been wonderfully happy,' she said, also in Spanish.

'No one could have been happier. I was indeed blessed, for not only were my family wealthy but I married the only man for me in the whole world. I was in love all my married life.'

'Perhaps that is why you look so young,' Joanna commented. 'I'm going to enjoy doing your portrait.'

'Ah yes, the portrait. I am to sit for you an hour each morning. Is that not so?'

Joanna answered vaguely, 'I'm not sure. Ramón said something about bringing me each morning and taking me back in time for lunch. If that is the arrangement it will suit me fine. An hour is long enough for you to sit.'

The Marquesa gave her a close look. 'You sound nervous, *pequeña*. I have seen much modern painting during my recent stay with relatives and I can assure you that I am very tolerant of it.' She leaned forward with a twinkle in her eye. 'I take it you do not want to paint me in the nude?'

'Oh no!' Joanna gasped, her face as red as a peony. 'Ramón could surely not have given you that impression?'

The Marquesa chuckled and her dark eyes twinkled. 'I am teasing you,' she admitted, obviously well pleased with Joanna's answers. 'I do not feel young since I was widowed. During my married life I enjoyed the tranquillity of the siesta hours, the quietness of indoors when everyone relaxed in the light dream-filled afternoon.' She smiled sadly. 'Now I do not sleep in the afternoon because then I cannot sleep at night. Even so, I have retained all my old ways. My husband was very interested in my clothes and complimented me often on what I wore. He adored me in my *robe de chambre*, which I made sure was very feminine with lots of lace and ribbons. I keep the last one he saw me in for special anniversaries of our life together.'

Joanna looked tenderly around the room and recalled the tall slim figure of Ramón's grandfather, a handsome virile man from whom Ramón had inherited many of his qualities. She could imagine the young Marquesa sitting at the exquisite little rosewood desk near the window. Her lovely long black hair would be loosened over her *robe de chambre* and the sunlight, muted by the iron grille and the heavy jasmine climbing round the window outside, would thrust fingers of beams stiffly spread through the indoor slats. In his robe, her husband would bend over her to plant a gentle kiss on the perfumed mass of dark hair, and so would begin their afternoon siesta together.

'Perhaps,' she suggested haltingly, 'perhaps I could do a portrait of you in your *robe de chambre* . . . the one your husband admired you in so much.' Her eyes alighted on a beautiful little gilded sofa upholstered in delicate silk damask. Then she looked at the Marquesa, who was smiling. 'On the sofa?'

The Marquesa laughed, a light laugh of gaiety. 'Why not? I have put on a little extra weight, but no matter. I shall wear my corset underneath. Now enough about me. Tell me all that has happened since we last met.'

The Marquesa showed a sudden girlish gaiety. She was full of sparkle and ready for gossip. Her dark eyes were keen and in no way impaired by old age as she looked with approval on the dainty figure of Joanna, taking in the shiny brown hair dressed naturally, the hint of make-up on the youthful skin, and the immaculate white sleeveless dress showing long slender legs placed demurely together. It delighted her to see that her guest had not lost her air of vulnerability. Yes, the English girl was enchanting with her swinging silk hair, eyes sparklingly alive and always smiling and pretty mouth tilted a little at the corners on the verge of laughter.

She inquired about Joanna's father, implying that her desire was only to hear that all was well with him. And Joanna obliged by speaking frankly of Nick's latest play and of the visit of Laurence and Candida. Contrary to Ramón's belief, the Marquesa showed a remarkable knowledge of what was going on around her. Much of what she knew she had been quick to grasp from the visits of friends, the occasional visit of the priest and her association with various charities. She still retained her sense of humour and they were both smiling when Ramón returned.

He seemed to stride in on a sweep of the mountain air, moving with the ease of relaxed muscles and wearing his brilliant delighted smile. Transferring his gaze from one to the other happy face, he cocked an inquiring eyebrow.

'You were saying?' he prompted, for conversation stopped as he entered.

The Marquesa obliged graciously. 'I have been catching up with the news.'

Ramón's eyes narrowed at his grandmother across the room. 'Most of which you already know I will warrant.' He was still smiling.

'That is so,' the Marquesa qualified. 'Your latest affair is with the golden-haired Englishwoman, an actress?' Her eyebrows lifted and she raised a small hand imperiously before he could speak. 'The Englishwoman being a guest of Señor Main. Am I correct?'

'You are,' Ramón conceded, unperturbed, as he strolled to one of the tall windows and turned around slowly to face the room. 'I can't think how you knew.' His face was in the shadow, his voice low and musical as always. And as always, it thrilled Joanna. There was no hint of subterfuge in his manner, merely a polite indifference.

The Marquesa ignored this. 'Why did you not bring her to see me?' she demanded.

He shrugged. 'For no reason. This time you were hoping it was different?'

'Is it different?' she queried dryly. 'Can it be that you have succumbed it last to golden hair and blue eyes?' Now it was her turn to narrow her gaze at her charming grandson.

'Or are you selecting a wife by the slow process of elimination?'

Ramón grinned and made a playful bow. 'I'm doing my best.'

The Marquesa made an impatient gesture with a flash of rings on a well-kept hand. 'Why is it that you do not attempt to settle down? Surely there is a woman somewhere who pleases you? You are high, wide and handsome. You have charm, a wealthy heritage and a spacious dwelling just waiting to be filled with a family. You are the most eligible of men.'

Again Ramón made a playful bow. He smiled at her indulgently, as one would at a sweet and silly child. 'And why am I the most eligible of men,' he said softly. 'Because of my worldly goods. I want no woman who has her eye on what I represent.' His brows raised on a wry grimace. 'I am surprised to hear my *abuela* speak of taking a wife in so practical a manner. Do you not wish me to fall in love first?'

The Marquesa looked in exasperation at his mocking smile. 'All right, make a joke of it. But you cannot fool me. This veneer of polish and arrogance which serves to keep you aloof and makes you so attractive to women covers a hidden volcano which some day some woman will rouse in you. When that happens beware, for you will never succeed in quenching it. You will be swept into another world. Your possessions, everything will be forgotten.'

Mildly, Ramón said, 'It would be most interesting to meet such a woman who will suit my fastidious taste. I cannot wait.'

'Neither can I. Yet it seems I must,' the Marquesa replied sadly. As always she was finding it impossible to be angry with her handsome, charming grandson for long.

Ramón contrived to look wise. 'You would not have me pick a wife at random? Even a man with my experience could make a mistake in seeking a wife without first consulting my heart?'

'Perhaps your heart is seeking a perfection that overrules all else?' The Marquesa had the light of battle in her eyes.

She looked angry and pleading in turns. 'No man is perfect, so why should you seek perfection?'

Gently, Ramón reminded her, 'I did not speak of perfection—you did. I would be the last man to regard myself as being worthy of the perfect woman.' He gave a sardonic grin. 'Although I have no doubt that Abuelo regarded you as the perfect woman.'

They exchanged swift glances which changed into smiles. The Marquesa spread out her hands with a hopeless gesture. 'What is one to do with you?' she exclaimed.

He consulted his watch. 'Bless us on our way, for we must leave now if Joanna is to be back for lunch,' he said, then paused. 'You have come to some arrangement about the portrait?'

'We have,' the Marquesa replied. 'We shall use this room and Joanna can begin immediately after mid-morning chocolate. With such an arrangement you can both have refreshment on arrival, for you will need it after the dusty car ride.' She then proceeded to fill in the details, to which Ramón listened comprehendingly with nods of his dark head.

Joanna had sat through it all with her hands folded demurely in her lap. Several times in the last few moments she caught Ramón's twinkling eye. How she loved him, and he would never know. Perhaps she had been too concerned about going back to London to notice that her feelings towards him had been changing during the last year. But he himself was unaware of it. She was hardly aware of it herself. It was extraordinary. She was not even sure how she loved him except that she wanted him to be happy, and that his hurt was her hurt.

They had taken their leave of the Marquesa and were crossing the courtyard when Ramón remarked casually, 'It occurred to me that, as an artist, you might be interested in some drawings on the walls of caves near here. I used to explore them as a child. We can walk in quite comfortably on a downward gradient. As a matter of fact I have just been there to see if they are still safe. Interested?'

He looked down at her so arrogant, so superbly at ease

with that tender mocking smile which made him such a pet that Joanna had to gather her wits and contrive a smile. 'You mean you'll take me there?' she queried with growing delight at the thought.

'Of course. If you are interested. It will only be a short visit as you are expected back to lunch,' he said.

Joanna hesitated. Lunch was not important to her, but he obviously wanted to be back on time. He could be in a hurry to return to Candida, for they were sure to have a date. She looked up at his lean vital features, the black head of thick springy hair, and was aware of the smile of heart-warming charm which, to her dismay, she was finding hard to treat coolly.

At last she said, 'I'd love to go, but shan't we need a torch?'

He drew one from his pocket and taking her arm escorted her around the back of the villa and through the grounds. The entrance to the caves was in a cluster of rocks at the top of an incline and situated below a ledge jutting out obviously to protect it. Ramón went first, dropping down the side of the ledge to the entrance before lifting his arms to swing Joanna down beside him. His hands stayed on her waist no longer than necessary to steady her, then he took the torch from his pocket and they moved forward. Joanna swayed as the sudden blackness blinded her after the clarity of light from the hot glaring sun. Ramón caught her and held her against him. The pressure of his hands on her shoulders increased, and he looked down into her face.

She noticed how dark his eyes were and the silkiness of the straight dark brows and eyelashes. For a moment the world stood still and it seemed he was about to kiss her.

Then his intentness broke into a smile and he said, 'Close your eyes for a moment.' She obeyed him, heard the click of the torch, then opened them again. 'Ready?' He released her slowly when she nodded and looked beyond the circle of light from the torch into the darkness. A gradual slope took them down into the depths and he kept a reassuring grip on her arm as they descended. The smell of earth rose dankly in her nostrils and the silence was uncanny. But the roof was high enough for them both to walk upright for quite some distance.

They rounded several sharp corners with the torch illuminating the way in a powerful beam. 'And here,' Ramón said, moving the torch beam up a wall, 'are the drawings.'

In silence, Joanna fixed her eyes on drawings hewn out of rock, all of them beautiful in line and suggested movement. 'They're wonderful,' she said in an awed whisper. 'One wonders what they would have looked like on canvas. That girl there carrying the platter to the young handsome god sitting on his throne—she's quite beautiful.'

Ramón concentrated the torch on the couple in question. 'They make a an interesting couple,' he said sardonically.

She wanted to say, two beautiful people, he so handsome, she so lovely and contented, both quite untouched by darkness and time. The profile of the young man was not unlike Ramón's and the girl could be herself.

Aloud, she said, 'I wonder if he's a prince. He looks rather like you.'

'I was thinking,' murmured Ramón, 'the girl looks like you, sweet and very young. Shall we go? No doubt there will be many other drawings further on which we have no time for now.'

He had ended by speaking rather brusquely as if he regretted the extra time it had taken to enter the cave. Joanna walked with him slowly up the steep gradient. His hand was on her arm, sending a current through her blood quickening her heartbeats. Long afterwards, Joanna remembered the beating of fragile wings in her breast, for scales seemed to drop from her eyes as they entered the bright outdoors again, slowly this time to assimilate the glare. It had taken these last brief moments alone with him to reveal the shattering secret of her heart. She loved Ramón, really loved him.

Love! Her breath caught in her throat and she pulled herself together shakenly. Never in her life had she dreamed that there could be a joy so exquisite and yet so frightening. Frightening because it was a fierce passion, exquisite because it was veiled in tenderness, in giving. She stole a glance at him as he flicked off the torch and putting it in his pocket, climbed up the steep side of the entrance to the cave and reached down a long arm to haul her up beside him. She thought, so much personality and charm is almost lethal when one loves the man. The most bewildering thing about it was the fact that he felt nothing. His fingers, now cool on her arm, were urging her forward back to the villa and the car. And he was so indomitably cheerful as he seated her in the car and slid in beside her that she hated herself for feeling like she did. She hated him too because he was so unaware of her wonderful discovery and how much more beautiful the world was around her.

What does it matter if he doesn't love me? she thought that night, snuggling unhappily into her pillow. I've proved something to myself anyway. I've grown up. I'll go with him to begin his grandmother's portrait in the morning, and it won't mean a thing.

Ramón was on time the next morning to pick her up. He put all her paraphernalia in the boot of his car and made casual conversation as he drove on his way. Joanna tried hard to listen, but somehow she found herself staring abstractedly ahead.

Suddenly Ramón stopped talking. 'Are you listening?' he asked politely.

'Yes. Yes, I'm listening. I . . . I'm sorry,' she murmured apologetically.

'I was saying about Las Jacarandas. I have decided to have it redecorated and restored.'

Joanna swallowed on a dry throat. So his home was to be made suitable for his bride! She had no idea what to say. The thought of him with Candida in his home, in his arms, was more than she could bear. She looked under her eyelashes at his strong lean hands on the wheel and knew just how gentle they could be. The silence stretched on.

'I have an idea that you are not paying attention,' he said in mild reproof.

She lifted her eyes to his profile and wished he would put on his usual speed. It was not like him to drive so casually. Besides, he was looking so . . . heartbreakingly handsome this morning with his dark eyes fixed on the hills ahead, the lovely mountains of his island home. The heat did not affect him. His smooth brown skin looked cool, his dark withdrawn gaze was now resting on the dusty ribbon of road unwinding through the windscreen. Soon the Villa Faustino would loom into view, browsing in the hot summer sun. The fragance of summer rode on the air. Never had the sky been more bluer, never the scenery more beautiful. Joanna, welcoming the soft caressing air on her face, felt that all the joy of living was fused into that moment in the profound silence. The soft hum of the car was as narcotic as Ramón's presence beside her. Her heart reached out to him on a wave of aching longing. Without him she was incomplete.

'I'm sorry,' she said apologetically at last. 'I'm afraid I was daydreaming. I'm sure you're doing the right thing in restoring the beauty of Las Jácarandas, if . . . if only for . . . for future generations.' Joanna bit her lip. The last two words she had babbled were replacements for three other words . . . his future wife. Only the words did not come out because of the pain in her heart at the thought. His swift intent gaze made her add hurriedly, 'What will you do while I'm at work on the portrait?'

Ramón swept the car round the last corner to the villa. 'I have much to do around the estate here and the workmen are still engaged at the back of the villa,' he said coolly. The white flower-clad columns of the villa came into view and Joanna realised that this, for Ramón, was his inherited home; not Las Jacarandas. That also was his home with all its beauty, but it was for his son when he married, his son and Candida's. The knowledge fell across the brightness of her day as ominously as the purple shadows flung across the grounds of the villa by the brightness of the sun. They seemed real to Joanna, who quelled a shiver as Ramón helped her from the car. She watched him unload her painting paraphernalia from the car boot. She would always remember this day; a day given to her by the gods from the few she had left with Ramón. A day of endless joy and sorrow.

He carried all her things to his grandmother's room and

she followed. As she made her way upstairs there was time to dwell upon the fact that she had fortunately grown up in the shadow of the Marquesa and was not therefore awed in any way by her presence. She liked the old lady very much and they had a bond between them—they both loved Ramón. Ramón's long strides had already taken him into the Marquesa's rooms when Joanna paused at an open window along the corridor to admire the view. The scent of climbing jasmine beneath her nose made her lean out blissfully and breathe it in before plucking off a blossom to tuck into the second buttonhole from the top in her dress.

Today she was wearing a sleeveless dress in fondant pink with a matching band around her head to keep the shining, swinging hair in place. It was a button-through dress like most of her summer dresses because it was useful to put a bikini underneath. She wore one underneath this morning for coolness. Had she travelled to the villa in her own car she would have stopped on the way back for a bathe at one of the little bays along the coast.

Ramón had already put down her easel and canvases by a small table which held her palette, paints and brushes, and he was greeting his grandmother courteously. After inquiring about her health, he seated Joanna near to a small table containing a tray of refreshments, and declined to take chocolate with them on the excuse of the pressure of work awaiting him in the library. He assured them that if he desired a drink he would order one to be brought to him there. As he was taking his leave he looked down for several moments on Joanna and his expression was suddenly gentle. Then, taking the spray of jasmine from her dress, he put it into his buttonhole, and with a mocking smile at her heightened colour, strode from the room.

The Marquesa said as Joanna served refreshments, 'Ramón is a blessing to me. He looks after the estate as efficiently as his grandfather did and I have no worries or responsibilities in that direction.'

Ramón's fondness for his grandmother was legendary, Joanna mused, and she refused to dwell upon his virtues. She nibbled her pastry, drank her chocolate and while the

Marquesa took a little longer to enjoy hers, stood up her easel and prepared her paints. Fortunately the Marquesa always scornfully ruled out even the minimum of fuss and did not take long to sit in the required position on the little gilded sofa backed by the soft grey silk damask-covered wall. She allowed her small feet to find their precise accustomed position on the tapestry-covered footstool and raised her chin at Joanna's request to give her face a clearance of shade. As she worked Joanna congratulated herself on suggesting that the Marquesa wore her *robe de chambre*. By doing so the old lady had a beautiful tender expression on her face, put there by the treasured memories of the happier times when she had worn it for her husband.

The return of Ramón an hour or so later marked the end of the first sitting. He lifted an appreciative brow at the portrait as Joanna proceeded to cover it up. She had stood it in a corner of the room until the next sitting, and she awaited his verdict silent and watchful.

'I like it,' he commented laconically, then patted her head and strode over to his grandmother, who had fallen asleep. He turned for a moment to smile across at Joanna before making the old lady more comfortable with pillows, and Joanna's heart rocked. She was rather taken aback by his sudden return and would have liked to have done something to her face beforehand. The room was like an oven, although the slats were across to lessen the glare of the sun. Beneath her dress her heart beat with a primitive rhythm which she was finding it difficult to subdue. His sudden appearance had acted like a forcing house on her emotions, and she knew that her love for him was the strong and powerful one which comes once in a lifetime. Of this she was sure. And with Ramón bending solicitously over his grandmother she was aware of another strange emotion; the emotion of jealousy, a swift jab, ignored and dismissed as soon as felt.

The paintbrushes were washed out and placed in a jar and she prepared to depart. In the courtyard the sun was relentless and Joanna thought wistfully of the bikini beneath her dress and cool beaches. She adjusted her shoulder bag to find that Ramón, instead of accompanying her to his car, was taking her around the back of the villa. He had his fingers around her elbow and the heat rose and fell around them. The contact made her quiver with the sensation of being at one, in perfect harmony with her companion.

'Are we going to the caves again?' she asked as she tried to keep up with his long strides. Perspiring still more, she looked up at him in exasperation. He looked so cool.

With an air of complete absorption in his thoughts he gazed down on her. He was smiling. 'You remember I told you that the workmen are still engaged at the back of the villa? I wish to show you what has been completed this morning.'

He led her through arbours of honeysuckle and cool green corridors of grape and roses, and there before them was the swimming pool. Cool blue water had been run into it, the metal rails leading down steps into the tiled pool shot splinters of light from the sun and from the high diving board.

Joanna stopped with delight and glowed up at him. 'It's super!' she cried. 'But ... but what does the Marquesa say?'

'Abuela is pleased, but not for herself. She knows it is for my family when I marry, and for myself of course.'

'So you've decided to marry?' Joanna looked somewhere in the region of his tie, thus avoiding his intent gaze.

He laughed. 'There is no deciding about it. I have always intended to marry some day. I am not the kind of man to lead a celibate life. Besides, I need an heir. My estates and enterprises on the island employ a considerable number of people and I want them to continue to do so.'

Joanna looked into the pool and imagined a fair head followed by several smaller ones. The little one at the front swimming arrogantly ahead would be as dark as Ramón, his father. Suddenly she had to obliterate their images from the water. Recklessly she began to unbutton her dress. 'I'm going into the water,' she cried.

To say that Ramón was startled was to put it mildly.

He gripped her wrist excruciatingly and his voice rasped, 'Are you mad? There are workmen about. Stop this nonsense at once!' he demanded.

It was not the kind of swimsuit she would have worn in his company, but at least she had aroused some emotion in him as she undid the last button to reveal the bikini and he released her wrist. Taking a bathing cap from her shoulder bag, she whipped off her headband and put it on. Oddly enough Ramón took the shock of her half naked body remarkably well. It was Joanna herself who took a little longer to recover from his dawning look of appraisal. Her body felt at fever heat and she was sure it would sizzle when she entered the water.

All would have gone well but for the workmen settling down to their packet lunches not far from the pool. They simply sat there, all six of them, and gaped as she reached the diving board. Six pairs of eyes glued themselves to her enchanting figure. Her bikini was more modest that most bikinis, but it faded into insignificance at the picture she made against the blue sky. If Rosita could see her now she would chortle with delight to see the unmistakable curves appearing in all the right places. Ramón's eyes swivelled from the spellbound workmen to Joanna's enchanting form, which would grace any holiday brochure so charmingly, and he glared, willing her to dive. Then, as if he could bear it no longer, he swivelled round and strode to the villa.

Joanna felt as though she was diving into a cool, green wood. The water lapped luxuriously around her warm limbs and she did several lengths of the pool. Ramón was there at the side of the pool as she reached it, and scowled as he helped her out. The huge towel was whipped around her and she was hurried unceremoniously towards the villa. The workmen had gone, coaxed indoors no doubt by Ramón on the bait of a meal.

Joanna looked up at his dark face as he hurried her indoors. 'Don't look such a crosspatch,' she cried. 'It was heavenly—just what I needed. May I use it again tomorrow after the sitting?'

'No, you may not,' he replied angrily. Almost carrying

her upstairs, he stopped at the door of a room and opened it. 'You will please dry yourself quickly and dress. The pool is not yet ready for use and the workmen will be there for several days yet.'

Her eyes danced. 'You thought I was going to dive in my birthday suit! Surely you know me better than that?' Laughter bubbled in her voice at the thought, then she sobered, realising that Ramón did not expect such levity even from a friend at his own expense. 'Oh, Ramón, I'm sorry.' She was immediately contrite. 'I didn't mean to upset you, honestly.'

Stiffly, he said with no softening of his expression, 'I think you forget where you are.'

Joanna furtively peered to her right and left along the corridor and was greeted by silence. Ramón's lips twitched at her wide-eyed look, then relaxed.

'No matter,' he assured her graciously. 'You will go now and change. I shall bring up your dress.'

'Oh, Ramón, you are a pet!' she cried, and reached up to place a butterfly kiss on his tanned cheek. It was a stupid thing to do, of course, for his sudden nearness brought a giddy reaction and her legs decidedly unsteady as she made her way into the room.

CHAPTER SIX

JOANNA was to remember afterwards that she had never felt so miserable as those days dating from the discovery of her love for Ramón. For years she had been fired with the idea of going back to London, and now that time was coming nearer she felt only a terrible heaviness in her chest, as if indigestion had stuck there like a brick. Ramón drove her to his grandmother's villa for the rest of the week, taking the narrow, winding roads swiftly with the expertness that she admired. She became familiar with the mountainous regions, sharp-peaked and barren, towering over deep gorges and the lush green of cultivated areas looming brilliantly against the sombre background.

She had suggested on her second visit that she could drive herself in her own car to the Villa Faustino, but Ramón had been very firm about it.

'I want to make sure that you finish the portrait before your visit to London,' he said mildly.

'You say that as if I'm going away for good,' she observed a little tartly. 'It's only a visit.' Accusingly her gaze swept over the vivid silk scarf tucked into the neck of his silk shirt, and the white linen suit. In the light through the car windows his smooth olive tanned profile was striking in its clear-cut outline and she longed to touch his cheek.

Ramón looked at her briefly as if he had almost forgotten that she was there. His thoughts were probably winging forth to later that day when he would be with Candida, she thought heavily.

He said with a touch of amusement, 'Do not be so vehement about it. Has the idea lost its appeal? Do you not wish to go?'

'Of course I do,' she answered shortly, and alarm rose in her like a tidal wave at the thought of leaving him.

'How long do you intend to stay in London?' he asked

carelessly as if it was of secondary importance to him how long she was away.

His sideways glance beneath a lifted eyebrow brought a blush to her cheeks and she said uncertainly, 'Nothing is settled yet. I shall probably leave when Laurence and Candida go.'

He made no reply and she wondered if his taking her daily to the Villa Faustino had any special significance. Then she dismissed the idea as being absurd. Nothing important happened during their second visit to the Villa Faustino, but Ramón was delivering her back home when he said, 'Bring your swimsuit with you tomorrow morning—the one-piece one. The workmen will not be there tomorrow and you can take a cool dip in the pool.'

The sun spilled down in flowing spun gold rays and the crimson, violet, primrose and blue petals of flowers were brilliant beacons to the bees circling around the garden when Joanna came down the next morning to breakfast.

Rosita followed her on to the terrace with fresh rolls and fragrant coffee. 'See that you eat a good breakfast,' she said, her gaze at Joanna's trim figure kind and probing. 'You're not relaxing as much as you used to do. Ask me, you're doing too much, off to paint until lunch, then gadding about with Laurence until the small hours. You were late again to bed last night, so your father says. He's in his study if you want him.'

'I don't.' Joanna poured cream in her coffee, stared out over the garden dreamily and said, 'It's going to be a heavenly day.'

Rosita waved an inquistive bee away from the bright blue of her dress and said tartly, 'I'd like to know where all this gadding about is going to get you. I've nothing against actors, but I don't think one is for you.' She emptied the breakfast tray and tucked it under a buxom arm, then went on darkly, 'Here you are letting the most exciting and eligible man on the island slip through your fingers because you haven't got the sense to trap him. Why, you could be a marquesa yourself instead of sweating on a portrait of one.'

She's right, Joanna thought despondently. Why don't I snap out of it and go and get my man? Excitement and depression washed over her in turn. It was the answer. And yet she knew she could not do it. Ramón would choose his own wife, and it would not be Joanna Main. She drank her coffee and watched as Rosita leaned over the terrace to have a word with her husband working in the garden. He was handing her a basket of cut flowers for the villa. His face was like lined copper, his eyes dark and brilliant as the morning. Joanna envied them their planned future with everything all neatly labelled.

She had finished her breakfast and was on her way to her room when a car swept up the drive. It was Ramón on time and she fled the rest of the way to her room, thankful that it was too early for either Laurence or Candida to put in an appearance.

'You are looking very beautiful this morning,' Ramón commented as he started the car..

Her dress, a flower print in very pretty muted colours forming wide bands across the fabric, had a square neckline with followed the pattern in cotton. Miserably, Joanna told herself that it was the dress he was admiring and said as gaily as she could, 'I've brought my swimsuit.'

He flashed her an odd look and swept the car forward, and no one could have accused him of dawdling that morning. Joanna found herself gripping the edges of her seat at intervals as they swept around corners at speed.

Finally, Ramón said evenly as he sped on to a strange road, 'We are calling at the convent of the Holy Child before we go on to the Villa Faustino. Today a garden party is being given for the poor and aged. I have a hamper to deliver.'

Joanna nodded, knowing that it would be filled with a generous offering of food and wine. Ramón was always so generous to the needy and she knew they loved him at the convent. The little Sisters came to collect gifts from the people of the island at intervals and Joanna always gave them refreshment when they called and they exchanged gossip.

They were driving now through a small pretty town of neat houses with well tended gardens, and small shops hiding behind shuttered façades. The convent was set in grounds of trees and shrubs and cloistered walks. In the courtyard stalls were being set up around the old well in the centre. Already some contained beautiful needlework and embroidery, home-made jams, honey and fruit.

Ramón had stopped the car outside the entrance to the courtyard and he helped Joanna out. In the shadow of the high walls the air was chill, and she quelled a shiver as Ramón's strong fingers closed with a protective warmth around her arm.

'Cold?' he remarked on a lifted eyebrow. 'The morning air is always a little chilly until the sun breaks through. Fortunately we shall be regaled with a glass of wine before we leave. The Mother Superior always insists upon it.'

She waited while he strode to the boot of the car to take out a large covered hamper. Then she followed him into the courtyard. There were many bobs and curtseys with murmurs of *buenos dias*, Señor Marqués, *señorita*, as they passed the neat black-robed figures at the stalls, and Ramón smiled with Joanna as they returned their greetings. Once across the courtyard, they passed along a loggia of vines and through an arched doorway into a cool hall of stained glass windows. Almost immediately one of the doors were opened and a black-robed young woman courteously bade them enter.

At the far end of the sparsely furnished room sat an elderly woman at a heavily carved table, writing. She put down her pen as they entered and swept forward in her black draperies to welcome them. Ramón put down the hamper and greeted her. Then she motioned them to leather-thonged chairs and poured them a glass of wine. Ramón gave Joanna her wine and smiled at her, that slow melting smile which warmed her as no wine had ever done, and her heart ached. She sipped it, feeling the warmth which Ramón's smile had begun spreading over her being, and listened to the conversation.

Apparently the convent did very well from the proceeds

of the garden parties and the Mother Superior was expecting another good day. Immemorially old and severely erect, she sat with an expression of repose upon her ageless face and smiled as she gestured with a blue veined ivory hand which Ramón kissed on parting.

Joanna told the Marquesa of the visit to the convent over mid-morning chocolate and the time went on wings. The old lady was clearly enjoying the change in her daily routine of Joanna's visit. Young company acted like a tonic on the aged and the hour she posed for her portrait went surprisingly quickly when engaged in conversation. Furthermore, her grandson was coming each day. True, she was a little apprehensive about his friendship with an English actress and would have preferred someone from his own circle of friends. Ever since Ramón had become of age there had been very strong pressure to bear upon him by all the members of his set who possessed daughters of a marriageable age. There had been high hopes on more than one occasion when Ramón had singled out a particular girl, and she reflected with a twinkle in her eye that he had done it with the same mocking perverseness that he had answered her query earlier on.

'You think it is different this time,' he had prevaricated. But he had not admitted to it being different. So there was hope that he would eventually pass over his present friendship with the actress and look elsewhere for his bride-to-be. The Marquesa's thoughts always began to be confused towards the end of a sitting as sleep claimed her. Her head gradually sank back against the cushions and she was not even aware of Joanna tenderly making her more comfortable. Ten minutes later, Joanna made her way to the swimming pool. She did not wait for Ramón to come and collect her, since he had spent a considerable amount of time with the Marquesa before leaving to work in the library on their arrival at the villa. Indeed, he had lolled elegantly in a chair while Joanna put in quite a number of brush strokes on the portrait.

He was there when she shed her dress to reveal a charming one-piece swimsuit in white jersey. Had he taken care to be at the opposite side of the pool? she thought, seeing him lying back on a lounger in his towelling robe. He had obviously been in the water, for his hair looked ebony wet. His eyes were closed.

Outwardly indifferent but inwardly seething at his lack of interest, Joanna made her way to the diving board and ignored him. She stayed in the water for ten minutes or more, swimming the length of the bath and floating leisurely. And not one glance did she spare for that long figure sprawled elegantly on his lounger. In the end she had to fight a instinctive desire to splash water all over him, and refrained after reminding herself of his many late nights out with Candida. It was so unlike him, though, to be tired. He was usually so indefatigable. Too irritable to dwell upon it for long, Joanna eventually made her way to the room Ramón had taken her to before to dress.

Later when she returned to the pool the lounger was empty and Ramón was leaning fully dressed against an archway, staring across the pool with a cigarette in his mouth. He straightened lazily upon seeing her and his expression was transformed into the smile both welcoming and charming.

His dark hair was curling as it dried, and in the sparkling reflection from the water of the pool, his arrogant features were decidedly striking, his smooth tanned face flatteringly without a blemish. Joanna avoided his eyes and refused to succumb to his undoubted charm. She was angry and it showed.

'Enjoy your sleep?' she asked with stormy eyes.

He lifted a provocative brow, put out his cigarette and lounged away from the supporting archway to stroll nonchalantly and unperturbed beside him. 'I was not asleep,' he answered coolly. 'I was thinking.'

This, she thought indignantly, was adding insult to injury! So he had deliberately ignored her presence. And because she wanted to hurt him for his indifference as he had hurt her, she said scathingly. 'The Marqués being deliberately rude to a guest he has invited to the pool? I can't believe it.'

The outraged virtue on his face stopped her as he confronted her. He was very angry. 'Have I not known you for most of your life?' he demanded. His face was set. 'And do we not share a special relationship, you and I, which is far removed from that of a host with a casual guest? Would you not say that we understood each other so well that there are times when words are not needed?' His dark eyes flashed. 'Answer me!' he insisted.

Joanna retreated a few inches, agreed, and quivered in the heat of his anger. His expression hardened as he drew in a tight breath.

'Then why,' he insisted, 'have you deliberately misconstrued my actions as being something which they definitely are not? The fact is that I had a problem which I needed to sort out on my own and the surroundings are ideal for that purpose. If I had intended to be rude to you would I have invited you here to the pool?' Arrogantly self-righteous, he added fiercely, 'Have you ever known me to be rude to anyone?'

Joanna's abashed gaze was lowered until her dark eyelashes rested on suddenly scarlet cheeks. Never had she seen him so angry. His nostrils flared and his teeth were tight. Bewildered, she could only think that his problem was to do with him and Candida. Poor Ramón! He was in love at last and like herself, he was finding it painful.

'Never,' she answered, and blushed more deeply beneath his fierce scrutiny.

Presently he moved closer and said in that rich deep voice which never failed to stir her, 'And how could I ever be rude to my Juana?' He held out his hand as he spoke and a petal-soft one was placed into it. The dark head bent and his cool lips caressed her hand. Achingly she wanted to run her fingers through the crisp dark hair and drown in his dark gaze. She had hurt him and in doing so had only succeeded in hurting herself. She made an effort to make amends.

'You were right,' she admitted as he lifted his head. 'Ours is a special relationship. Why else should I be annoyed because you ignored my presence at the pool? The truth is I wanted you to notice that I had put on the swimsuit you wanted. Women do strange things ... like reacting differently when in men's company. Now do you see?'

'I see,' said the Marqués. 'I see that I do not understand women.'

They were back on a friendly plane by the time the car was speeding on the return journey. Joanna was hatless and her silky hair lifted in the slight breeze through the car window. It was almost midday and the sun was hot upon the road unwinding in front of them, the occasional white villa in gardens brilliant with flowers. Now and again the windows of a villa high in the hills would react to the sun like molten fire, blinding the eyes.

Ramón's deep baritone voice made comments to which she half listened, being more concerned with the man himself. It seemed to her that she had always known his air of distinction, the slow quizzical smile which lighted his dark eyes, eyes which looked into hers so intently that there could not be a corner of her mind closed to him. His dark hair was rumpled by the breeze, but his careless arrogance made everything about him correct and never out of place. These brief interludes with him revealed only too clearly the tremendous, incredible thing that had turned her placid pool of existence into a raging torrent of emotion. She found herself uttering any available platitude that came to mind because she was afraid of betraying herself beneath those searching eyes. He really was an incredible man, for he had survived many of her English ways and customs so alien to his aristocratic Spanish unbringing. No doubt he would accept more alarming things with equal calm from Candida. If only it had been herself that he was in love with! However, it was too late now, and with this depressing thought Joanna came on the reassuring sight of the villa.

Candida came to the car immediately it stopped and Joanna flitted away to leave her alone with Ramón. But not before she had seen him give Candida the same absorbed look, the same interest, which his congenital courtesy brought to all contacts, however brief. Candida had swept gracefully forward, a vision of loveliness skilfully applied, her golden head gleaming in the sun. She greeted Ramón softly in Spanish and went on in the foreign tongue in an enunciation as pure as that of Joanna herself, who followed the drift of her words easily. Ramón was very pleased indeed as he greeted her. Candida had certainly lost no time in learning a little of the language of her intended, Joanna thought, hurrying indoors before the serenity of her own face cracked with the emotion of pain lurking beneath.

Once in her room she washed and swiftly changed into denim shorts and sleeveless top with the waiting lunch in mind. Rosita did not like being kept waiting when the meal was ready. Lunch was served on the terrace, and to her surprise, Joanna was the first down. Ramón had gone and the villa seemed strangely empty without his car in the courtyard. Sadly she stood looking at the view. It was too beautiful for words, she thought. The air was crystal clear, the sea and sky a translucent blue and each deep breath was taking in something rarefied and pure. Today the beauty of her surroundings took on a poignant loveliness. A gull swooped overhead in pure poetry of motion and winged out to sea; a flash of white in the sun. With the same cataclysmic suddenness Joanna was aware of emotions which hitherto had been dormant; deeper, more disturbing than any she had known, more profound, as if she had been plunged into another world other than her own.

She was conscious suddenly of Laurence at her side. 'I'd like to paint this view before I go,' he said.

He turned to smile at her, his dark grey eyes quizzical. Before she could reply Candida appeared with Nick. Joanna, giving Laurence a smile of acknowledgement, turned to greet the other two. Her father gave her an amused smile as he saw her with Laurence and without being able to help it she blushed. He probably thinks I'm falling in love with Laurence, she thought, as she sat down at the table. A deep emotion touched her, surprising her by its depth. It would be awful if Laurence were to fall in love with her now that she knew she could never feel the same way about him. So far her life had been straightforward and uncomplicated. But that deep awareness of another world far different from her own present one was now almost tangible, more tangible than it had been a few moments ago before Laurence had arrived on the terrace.

Laurence sitting so close beside her meant nothing in the sudden stricken intensity of her yearning for Ramón. Her glance across the table at Candida illuminated a different facet of the woman Ramón loved. Something about her golden hair, blue eyes and arresting personality had captured his heart. To him, she was both potentially exciting and desirable. And poor Joanna saw that as Candida was to Ramón so Ramón was to herself. Through the years when Ramón had taken her arm in a friendly gesture to assist, she had felt nothing more than the warm comforting pressure of his brown hand—a strong firm grasp, entirely impersonal. But the discovery of her love for him had changed all that. It could be that the glimpses of his brilliant mind, the laughter and wit he had shared with her, the undeniable beauty of his voice, the way the sun slanted on his handsome head when he stood arrogant and very sure of himself, as though his kingdom was within himself, and finally the shattering impact of his gaze, had resolved itself into the whole being of the man, the exciting, devastating Ramón.

They all chatted in a desultory fashion during the meal, silently revelling in Rosita's speciality, a niçoise salad, garnished with anchovies and set on a bed of lettuce. Chilled with ice, it was both delicious and satisfying. As usual Nick was abstracted and Joanna accepted his silences as being part of him. Laurence and Candida were learning to accept them also. There was no doubt about it, Candida and Laurence were a charming couple and they fitted into the household remarkably well; so well that instinct told Joanna how easy it would be to regard Laurence as more than a friend. The beauty of their surroundings, their lotus-eating existence, added to the spell in which, Joanna knew, she would find it fatally easy to accept second best.

She realised suddenly how rapidly she was growing up. The Joanna of a week or so ago would hardly have thought on those terms. But her love for Ramón had awakened her, she knew that it had. She had changed. Would her father notice? Half the time he was oblivious of her presence. But it was only one of the things about him that she loved and understood. Seated opposite to him at the table, she knew by the changing expressions on his face that his mind was occupied and alert with some work in hand.

He returned to them suddenly and said, looking at Joanna, 'Didn't I hear Ramón's car just now?' Joanna nodded and he clicked his fingers. 'Of course! You've been to do that portrait of the Marquesa. Why didn't he stay to lunch?'

It was Candida who answered. She made a gesture with a flash of scarlet nails matching the vivid scarlet flowers on her black cotton trouser suit.

'He was in a hurry. He has a business appointment this afternoon.' She paused and looked at Joanna. 'How's the portrait of the Marquesa going?'

Joanna helped herself to coffee. 'Very well.'

Candida yawned prettily. 'I don't know how Ramón manages to be up so early in the morning after a late night. The man is indefatigable! I heard his car at the crack of dawn this morning coming to collect you.'

Joanna felt a stab of jealousy, an unbearable pain at the thought of Ramón bringing Candida home in the small hours after their evening out, and ignored it. 'I wouldn't say eight-forty-five is exactly the middle of the night,' she said without rancour. 'Daddy is up very often at six in the morning to do his writing.'

Candida shrugged. 'I'm afraid I've never been an early riser. Tell me about the Marquesa. What's she like? Some of those old Spaniards are old dragons clinging on to their ancient beliefs.'

'The Marquesa is a dear and I love her,' Joanna admitted serenely.

'Really?' Candida put down her coffee cup and looked interested. 'Tell me more.'

But Joanna was reluctant to enlarge upon her last remark. For one thing she resented the reference to the old lady who belonged to a world where present-day values did not exist. And that world, since Ramón was a part of it, beckoned. It was a world in which she took part with a familiar sense of expectancy and pleasure; a world where she shed all worries and conflicting thoughts . . .

'You're talking about one of Joanna's friends.' It was Laurence who spoke observing both charming faces with a sort of tender tolerance. 'I have no doubt that she must be a charming lady, and I'd like to see the portrait when it's finished.'

Candida, still rather taken aback at what he had said, smiled rather tightly. She said slowly, 'I shall go one better and see the Marquesa herself. I have only to ask Ramón to take me.'

The remark annoyed Joanna faintly. She wanted to point out that she had not asked for their approval of the portrait which Candida was so ready to give. But the warmth of Laurence's regard and Candida's dazzling smile disarmed her.

'I'm sure he will,' she told her evenly with no more than a polite interest, a defence against the power to hurt which Candida's words, however unintentionally, had. To her relief her father joined in the conversation with a request for Laurence's company after lunch to discuss the now finished play, and they talked about the forthcoming opening in London. To Joanna London seemed a long way off, and the prospect of leaving Ramón was a bleak one. She was only just beginning to realise how much she had depended upon his friendship. But, if her love for him was so deep, she supposed that the further away she went from him the better.

They were alone on the terrace, for Nick had taken Laurence to discuss the play. Joanna pushed back her hair, feeling warm after her meal and a little on edge. A bathe in the sea would be very welcome. Candida reclined in her chair with a cigarette.

Joanna said, 'I'm going down to the beach. It seems Laurence will be with Daddy for the rest of the afternoon. What about you?'

Candida thoughtfully tapped the ash from her cigarette

into an ash tray on the table, and shrugged. 'I'm at a loose end this afternoon as Ramón is all tied up for the rest of the day with commitments. Suppose we ask Rosita for a picnic basket, and we can go down on the beach? We can leave Laurence a note to join us later if he wants to.'

Joanna went to ask Rosita to put up a picnic tea for two and went to her room for her bathing things. When she returned to the terrace with the picnic basket Candida was ready in a black and white beach ensemble and a smart white turban over her blonde hair. Her lovely limbs were gloriously suntanned, and she was more relaxed than Joanna when she slipped into the car beside her.

'Looking forward to your visit to London?' she asked as Joanna set the car in motion and they slid from the villa downhill.

'Yes. It's kind of you to invite me to share your flat,' Joanna answered. 'I hope I won't be in the way.'

'I'm going to enjoy your company, and I'm sure all the men will.'

Joanna drove carefully between palms and bougainvillaea on the sloping white road and turned on to the highway. 'I suppose you know lots of men,' she said. 'I'm afraid I'm not very bright with them. I've met very few Englishmen.'

'Anyone like you, wide-eyed, willowy and silky-haired, doesn't have to be bright,' said Candida. 'Your innocence gives you the look of someone waiting for her knight in shining armour, and believe me, the men will only be too eager to oblige.' Candida flashed a searching glance from blue eyes. 'Tell me, is Laurence your shining knight in armour?'

'No, he isn't.' Joanna surprised herself that she could say it so firmly. 'Why do you ask?'

'Because if that's so I must warn you to be careful about monopolising him. Laurence is no boy. He's a grown man.'

'Do you mean I'm a child?'

'No, not exactly a child. But singularly untouched. You're a creature from another world with all the appearance of it. A little behind the force of emotions of the present generation.'

'And?' Joanna said coldly.

'Most men now consider women fair game and they can never resist a virgin like yourself. I know because I've experienced it. Men haven't changed, they never will. They're all endowed with the same fundamental human emotions struggling underneath to get out. Laurence is no exception. His charm is not congenital like Ramón's. It's a studied charm which one has to acquire to be a successful actor. Some actors are born with it, others have to acquire it.'

Joanna said quietly, 'Are you trying to turn me off Laurence?'

Candida laughed. 'No, I'm not. But I'm older than you and I've seen more of the world. Laurence's first love is the stage. Everything else takes second place.'

'Thanks for the warning.' Joanna was flippant. 'Never marry an actor. Will the stage always take first place with you?'

Candida's eyes softened and deepened. 'Not since I've met Ramón,' she answered.

Joanna could not say in truth that she enjoyed that afternoon out with Candida. Their conversation in the car had left a sting behind which rankled. But once in the water with the shimmering sea rippling around her, she relaxed. Her body, flexed and sinuous, revelled in the warmth of the caressing waves and the feeling of freedom. Later, they stretched out luxuriously on their beach towels and slept. During their picnic tea, with Candida doing most of the talking, Joanna responded politely, at times even with animation. But she was happy when they returned to the villa and even a little relieved. The question of why Candida should warn her off Laurence was still unanswered. Was she the man-eating type who wanted every man for herself, or had she been sincere? As they came in sight of the villa, Joanna's tranquillity returned. What did it matter anyway? If Laurence was so deeply interested in his career then he could not be much of a menace in the love game.

CHAPTER SEVEN

DINNER that evening was a happy meal. Laurence talked of amusing experiences in his short acting career, and watching her father's reaction, Joanna was aware that Laurence was a man whom most people instinctively liked. After dinner, however, she felt a need to get away; to be by herself. As it happened there were no problems. Immediately after dinner Candida went to her room to write letters and Nick drew Laurence on to the terrace to play a game of chess.

Once when she was a child, Joanna had been caught in a violent thunderstorm in the hills and she had stumbled to one of the cave dwellings in which lived an old woman known as Tia Rosalba by the local people. People went to her for advice and she knew many cures of ailments with herbs which she mixed herself. Her face was as brown and wrinkled as a walnut and she smoked a pipe. The children of the village had given her a wide berth, regarding her as a witch, but Joanna's terror of the storm had been far greater than that of Tia Rosalba, and she had slunk into the warm cave drenched to the skin.

Wisely, Tia Rosalba had thrown her a towel and had not approached her small, quivering form. Then she had motioned her to the fire to give her hot soup and bread. Well over eighty now, Tia Rosalba was still there in her cave dwelling and Joanna had visited her regularly through the years with gifts of food. She had never forgotten that awful day in the storm, and the old woman's kindness to her.

This evening, in an effort to get away from it all, Joanna went to the kitchen and filled a basket to take to Tia Rosalba. It was a beautiful evening for a walk into the hills, and the caves, frightening and eerie on that day of the storm, were now bright with flowers.

Tia Rosalba was sitting at the door smoking her pipe

when Joanna arrived and rose to her feet to receive the basket. Then, leading the way indoors, she bade Joanna sit down. The room, a rather large one, was a bedsitter with the kitchen in one corner. It was spotlessly clean, with a hand-embroidered cover on the bed and pictures on the whitewashed walls made from pressed wild flowers which Tia Rosalba had done herself.

Joanna watched the claw-like hands drawing aside the white linen cover on the basket, knowing that Tia Rosalba's old eyes would glow at the sight of the plump chicken, the large fruit cake and all the other delectable goodies inside. There was no need to say why she had come. Tia Rosalba would know. She always did. She sat down in her chair holding the pipe in her mouth with one hand and supporting the elbow with her other.

The silence which ensued was very relaxing, and after a few moments of studying her, Tia Rosalba rose to pour out a glass of her home-brewed wine which she gave to Joanna.

'You are pale, *niña*, and beset with problems,' she said, putting a hand on Joanna's slim shoulder. 'The world beckons to you like it does to the young, yet you are unwilling to go. You need the widening of your horizons before you settle down. Go over the water. We shall miss you, but we must not be selfish. With our Spanish customs to guide you you will not go wrong.'

So that was that, Joanna thought as she wended her footsteps homeward. She was going to London, but she did not get the bit about the Spanish customs. At a bend on the sloping path she turned to wave to Tia Rosalba, who stood at the door of her cave to lift a blue-veined hand in farewell. Pausing now and again to drink in the beauty of the view bathed in the molten glow of the sunset, or to exchange a dignified greeting with other cave-dwellers as she passed, Joanna found the tensions inside her relaxing a little.

As she walked Joanna's thoughts began to take shape. What did she know of love in any case? She could be infatuated with Ramón; with his lithe figure, intent gaze, quick, graceful movements and his indescribable arrogant air of power and authority. The big car slid almost noiselessly to a halt beside her. She had reached the foothills and the main highway, half way home. She swung round, startled, and the colour rushed into her face.

'Ramón! How you startled me. I never expected to see you.' Joanna looked at him as he swung open the car door, her blood racing. But the frenzied beating of her heart was not fright. Caught off guard thinking about him, her blush had been a guilty one. Seeing him again it was all she could do to hide the fact.

'I'm sorry I frightened you,' he said. 'What are you doing out alone at this hour?' He leaned across her to see that her door was closed and for a few seconds he was close against her. An electric ripple rode along her nerves, a purely instinctive reaction to his masculinity which she tried in vain to suppress. Then he straightened with his arm on the car wheel. Silhouetted against the light from the far window of the car, his tanned face held an angular beauty. His body was erect with the suggestion of vitality held in check.

Calmer now although her pulses still leapt at his nearness, she braved his intent gaze. 'I've been to see a friend in the caves.'

'On foot?' he said. 'Why not on the pony or in the car? It is late, or have you not noticed? When you are in love time ceases to exist. Does it not?'

She froze at the anger in his voice. 'I don't know what you mean,' she said.

He gave a snort of disbelief. 'When a young woman goes to see Tia Rosalba the answer is only too clear. You are in love with Laurence?'

'I don't have to answer that. You can be so charming, Ramón. Please don't be beastly,' she pleaded.

He tossed her a glittering look. 'Am I being beastly because I am stating fact? When one feels as ...' He stopped abruptly.

'Go on,' she insisted. 'When one feels what? I shall understand.'

'I am sure you will not. I was going to say that a Spaniard feels more deeply about ... the freedom of women to make fools of themselves.'

'I am not making a fool of myself,' Joanna said quietly. 'I am doing exactly what you did at the swimming pool at the Villa Faustino that day—sorting out my problems. Of course I find Laurence attractive, but I'm not mad about him.'

She glanced at him beneath her lashes. The line of his jaw was set, heartbreakingly appealing in its rigidity and masculine strength. No wonder she loved him. He cared for things that happened, cared for people. It was one of the charms which made him so very attractive to women, particularly herself.

'What you feel for Laurence,' he stated cynically, 'is infatuation to an overpowering degree. He is a blond Englishman of the kind you have always dreamed of.'

Joanna was near to tears. 'I know you think I'm young and silly. All right, laugh. But it isn't what you think at all.'

'I am not laughing at you,' he said soberly. Looking at him swiftly, Joanna saw that he was serious. 'Are we friends again?'

He was smiling again, mocking, amused, and undeniably attractive, masking all the vitality beneath the lazy exterior, the absurdly dark, thick eyelashes veiling a keen, arrogant gaze. She thought despairingly, what chance has a mere girl against that battery of charm?

He started the car and it leapt away to his bidding. 'Now that we have become friends again we can stop to toast our renewed friendship in wine,' he said firmly in a voice which brooked no denial. He turned his head and smiled at her, that slow melting before which she was powerless, and she nodded agreement. Smiling back, Joanna was beginning to feel better than she had all evening.

Their destination was a place in the hills overlooking the sea with black beams, white walls and rough-hewn wooden tables and chairs. The wine, a local muscatel, was served from barrels by white-jacketed waiters. They were served with glasses of amber wine and a plate of small sweet almond biscuits, and raised their glasses to each other. The next hour went on wings as the wine spread fire through Joanna's veins. They conducted a cool, conventional conversation, or rather Ramón did, until he said,

'And what do you intend to do in London?' His look was direct, challenging, and Joanna knew that he expected an answer.

Awkwardly, she said, 'I told you—I want to see everything there is to see.'

'And after that?'

'I don't know,' she admitted. 'I love the life here, of course. What happens next will be a matter of course.'

'Yes,' Ramón said slowly, looking out to the distant sea covered now with the purple shadows of late evening. 'You are right. We shall miss you.' He was silent for so long that Joanna wished with torturing longing to know what lay behind the set muscles of his face.

'I suppose you will stay here as always. After all, it is your home,' she said on an enforced lightness.

At first it seemed he had not heard her and the silence stretched on. Then he said, 'Naturally this is my home. However, I can only speak for the moment. Unforeseen things can happen. On the other hand, many people here depend upon me for a living.'

For a moment Joanna was tempted to ask him outright about his feelings for Candida. But it simply was not done, not with the Marqués, and for all his tender teasing, he remained very much the monarch of all he surveyed on the island. His thoughts, his intentions would always remain a closed book to be opened only by himself.

When he looked at his watch and said, 'I think we had better go now. It is getting late,' she stood up reluctantly, and followed him from the cosy atmosphere with smiles and nods for the people who wished them a quiet, '*Buenos dias*,' as they passed their tables. More than one pair of feminine eyes rested upon Ramón. His virile good looks and easy grace drew them like a magnet and Joanna not only felt a strange new delight in being with him, she also knew the delight of being a woman. Laurence had been the instigator of her growing up, but Ramón's charm, her love for him, had made her aware for the first time of her own vulnerable femininity. It was exciting and heartbreaking at the same time.

The long gleaming car throbbed into silence outside the Villa Rosario and Candida greeted them eagerly from the terrace. She wore a white housecoat with a gold scarf around her slender throat which emphasized the gold of her hair. A bracelet on her wrist caught the light as she went eagerly towards them. To Joanna her pretty gestures were slightly theatrical, but they made her an arresting personality.

'My dear Joanna,' she cooed in her warm throaty voice. 'How naughty of you to go out without telling me! And you're very late. Laurence and your father have gone to bed. And Ramón, what a lovely surprise to see you. I thought you were all tied up with business today?' Her voice had softened into a caress as one white hand fluttered on Ramón's sleeve. Her eyes were the dark blue of the evening sky. How could any man resist her? Joanna found herself thinking. Who would want to? Ramón was smiling down at her and Joanna had the feeling that they knew each other well, so well that she felt outside their conversation.

Ramón was saying, 'I was on my way home when I met Joanna. I trust you had a nice day.'

'On my own? You must be joking! I missed you. Do come in for a drink before you go.' She smiled up at him cajolingly, and Ramón shook his head as she slipped a hand under his arm to draw him forward.

'No drink, *gracias*. I had one with Joanna.'

Ramón smiled down at her and consequently Candida's frown was fleeting.

'It was naughty of you to keep her out so late,' she said softly, her blue eyes on Joanna's wide-eyed gaze. 'She's only a child, so slender, with that lovely complexion which is in danger of being spoiled with late nights. You look tired, Joanna—do go to bed. I can see Ramón to his car.'

Considering that the car was only a few yards away it was clear that Candida wanted to be rid of a third party, and Joanna fled after bidding them goodnight. It was silly to allow such a thought to hurt. Yet hurt it did. Was it because she loved Ramón so desperately? Or was it because of Ramón's total absorption in Candida? He had hardly lifted his head as Joanna had taken her leave of them—that had hurt most of all. She sat on her bed for a long time trying to subdue the riot of emotion inside her. How clever Candida had been to draw attention to her own youth, thus encouraging Ramón to continue treating her as a child. What weapons had she to use against the experience of the older woman? It seemed that her own love for Ramón was something she had to kill, for an emotion so powerful could only lead in time to the point of no return.

Joanna awoke early. In spite of the events of the previous evening she had slept dreamlessly through the night. The early morning mist was slowly lifting to reveal a clear and bright day. She stood at the window to breathe in the crystal clear air and already her alert mind was making plans for the day. This morning she would put on her sunglasses while she was with Ramón in the car. Behind them she would feel protected, more able to assemble her defences. For her love for him was still real enough. Even in the shelter of her own room, she was as fully aware of his impact on her senses, terribly conscious of the strong attraction he held for her.

Uncertain what to wear, she decided upon a simple button-through dress of blue denim with a camisole top, filling in the neckline with a triple row of coloured beads. With it she wore a trim little jacket which converted it into a demure suit. At least, she thought with satisfaction, her slim figure and long golden legs had an exciting blend of extreme youth combined with a touch of elegance.

She saw Candida's slender figure almost as soon as she stepped on to the terrace for breakfast. She was wearing a cream linen dress with broad bands of colour around the flared skirt and waist. A matching triangle of material was tied over her golden hair. She had been standing at the far end of the balcony and she moved forward as Joanna appeared.

'I've stolen a march on you this morning,' she said softly.

'So I see.'

'Surprised?' Candida laughed soundlessly. 'I told Ramón you would be.'

Joanna sat down at the table and Candida took a place opposite to her. She sat directly in the sun's rays which gave her face a sharp angular beauty. Just like the spotlight on any stage, Joanna reflected. Candida's face was the kind which stood out well in any strong light. She wondered why she was up so early, and dressed too, not in her usual housecoat which she kept on during the mornings for her sessions going over the play with Nick and Laurence.

Rosita came with the breakfast tray, raised an eyebrow at Candida and ambled away again.

'You're not curious why I should be up so early?' Candida said, looking fixedly at Joanna over her glass of fruit juice.

'Why are you up so early?' Joanna asked judiciously. 'I would have said it was something important.'

They held each other's gaze for a moment, Joanna's curious, Candida's veiled. 'Exactly what Nick said when I asked for a morning off from play-reading.' She smiled. 'I'm going with you and Ramón to the Villa Faustino. I knew Ramón would have taken me sooner or later, but I want to meet the Marquesa.'

Something dark brushed against the brightness of the morning for Joanna. It was clear that Candida was letting her know of the bond between her and Ramón. It showed in the movements of her body, the look in her blue eyes. Joanna saw it as a subtle warning of ownership, of indisputable possession which she could not ignore, and in which she had no part. If she had not been engaged in painting the old lady's portrait, she would insist upon Candida going alone with Ramón, knowing that they would both prefer it.

Instead, she said evenly, 'You'll like the Marquesa. She was very beautiful in her youth and she's still good-looking.' Joanna chatted brightly in case Candida regarded her silence as being redolent of disapproval of her going with them. And then Ramón was there, leaving his car and coming on to the terrace in his long strides. He was in great good humour, glowing with health and vitality and masculine charm. Joanna's heart turned over when she looked at him.

Candida was seated in front of the car with Ramón, leaving Joanna to sit in the back. She sat immediately behind Ramón and she had eyes for him alone. During the journey she realised how utterly, to the exclusion of all else, he had begun to absorb her. It frightened her. And yet she had known that love would be like this when it came; the warning leap of her heart when he was near, the tortured breathlessness when his eyes became entangled with her own.

The Marquesa greeted Candida graciously and soon they were all chatting over mid-morning chocolate. The old lady showed a remarkable knowledge of London and the theatres, having paid visits there with her husband years ago. What her real opinion of Ramón's latest affair was she kept hidden behind her bright dark eyes, and Joanna noticed that her look was very thoughtful when Ramón took Candida off to see over the villa.

It was more than an hour and a half later, with the Marquesa already asleep and her portrait put away for the day, that Joanna decided to go in search of Ramón and Candida. She made her way as usual around the back of the villa to the swimming pool. They were not there, and Joanna thought longingly of the swimsuit beneath her dress. Surely there was time for one little dip in the pool. The water looked so inviting and she was sticky with the heat. Swiftly she unbuttoned the dress, put on her bathing cap and plunged into the water.

The next ten minutes were sheer bliss and she reluctantly left the water, feeling tingling fresh, to see Ramón coming towards her from the direction of the villa. As she ran to meet him her bare wet feet slid along the rest of the distance between them and she was catapulted into his arms. Instantly, Ramón had reached out for her, his arms hauling her close. His strong, lean body was hard, and the unpremeditated contact startled her. The strength of his hold, his nearness, rippled along her nerves and her legs felt weak.

Then he had released her as swiftly as he had caught her, and she said rather breathlessly, 'Thanks. You saved me from a nasty fall. I know I should have been more sedate.' Suddenly a hand flew to her mouth in dismay as she saw the dark patch of wet on his light suit where he had clasped her against him. 'Your suit, Ramón! It's wet.'

He smiled. 'No matter. It will dry and I shall not catch my death of cold. Go and dress, then come to the library.'

Her answering smile was sweet. It was impossible not to love him at that moment, as he stood there lithe and supple, his dark eyes laughing down at her.

'Joanna, you look as fresh as a spring morning.' Candida gave her warm, deep-throated laugh as Joanna joined her and Ramón in the library of the Villa Faustino. 'Ramón tells me that you've been in the outdoor pool. What a pity I didn't bring my swimsuit along. I could have joined you.'

Her trained voice seemed to leave an echo in the room, and Joanna was aware of her sharp glance. Candida was sitting smoking for all the world as though she was already mistress of the villa, while Ramón was looking from one to the other with his charming smile.

'There will be other times for you to use the pool,' he said, and looked at his watch. 'When Joanna has had some wine I think we had better start back. I have several appointments this afternoon.'

Candida's mouth pouted. 'Oh, Ramón! Not again?' she wailed, and stubbed out her cigarette with some force into an ash tray on a nearby table. 'Another day on my own! Really, this is too bad!'

Ramón was unperturbed. 'You can spend the time preparing for dinner with me this evening. I am giving a small party for some business colleagues and you are all invited. I have already told Nick.'

He was about to pour wine from a decanter on the heavily carved table which also served as a desk for business purposes when Joanna stopped him.

'No wine, thank you, Ramón. I'm quite ready to return when you are,' she said.

Ramón would not stay for lunch when he dropped Joanna

and Candida off at the villa and he bade them *adios* until the evening. Nick and Laurence were on the terrace enjoying an aperitif before lunch. Laurence looked at them idly swirling the ice around in his drink.

'We were beginning to think you'd decided to lunch out,' he said, looking at Joanna in her blue denim dress, her face glowing with health, her silky hair gleaming in the sun. 'How was the portrait?'

'All right,' she answered, and caught her father's eye. 'You didn't say that we were going to dinner with Ramón this evening.'

Nick tossed off the rest of his drink. 'Didn't I? Well, we are,' he grinned. 'Now be a lamb and tell Rosita we're ready for lunch.'

The meal progressed easily. There was always plenty to talk about, mostly plays and entertainment in general. They were at the coffee stage when Laurence said, 'Well, how did you get on with the Marquesa, Candida?'

'You're wondering if she approved of me?' Candida's blue eyes gleamed strangely. 'I'm sure she did. We have much in common. The Marquesa knows as much about the London theatres as I do. She's a very sweet person.'

'I agree with you there.' Nick leaned forward with a lighter for Candida's cigarette. 'So you enjoyed yourself?'

Candida's eyes were full of dreams as she blew out a thin line of cigarette smoke from red lips. 'I did immensely. May I go again tomorrow?'

Nick lighted his own cigarette. 'I'm sorry, but we did agree to work until lunch each day on the play. After all, there isn't much time left. You'll soon be going back to London for rehearsals there.'

Candida could be very charming when it suited her and her smile at Nick was particularly so. 'You're right, of course. I shouldn't have asked.' Her smile now included Joanna and Laurence. 'I suppose you two young things will be going out this afternoon in the heat. I shall wash my hair in preparation for this evening.'

'Are we going out?' Laurence, in his casual clothes, lightweight slacks and open-necked shirt, looked very much at home as he asked the question. A cigarette burned steadily between his brown fingers.

Joanna laughed, welcoming the break. 'Why not? Unless you want to wash your hair in preparation for the party this evening?' Her eyes twinkled mischievously at his uplifted brow. Laurence was a welcome distraction.

Darkly, he said, 'I'll let you know what I think of that remark later.'

The air was clear and sparkly with the sun dazzling on every leaf when they set off for a walk in companionable silence. Joanna had not changed. She still wore the blue denim dress minus the jacket and the slight breeze lifted her silky hair. Laurence glanced down at the enchanting curve of her cheek, his grey eyes intent. She was the only girl he had ever met who could stir his pulses and whip his blood into desire for her. All the other women of his acquaintance faded into insignificance beside her. And Joanna was telling herself obliquely that whatever leaning she had towards this big blond Englishman was gone, and this walk with Laurence confirmed it.

They were making for the shade of the hills where narrow green paths meandered among trees giving shade. Now and then there were glimpses of splendid views of sea and sky, banana plantations and villas clinging to slopes.

'Do you think Daddy's play is going to be a success?' Joanna asked.

'I can't see it being anything else. A play by Nick Main will always draw the crowds. That's why I'm so grateful to him for giving me this chance, a chance in a million to make good.' Laurence smiled down at her wryly. 'I owe him an awful lot, you know. I would do anything for him or you.'

'That's nice of you.' Joanna turned a glowing face up to his and he thought she looked entrancingly pretty. 'I wish you wouldn't think like that, though. I'm sure Daddy doesn't think that way. You'll find he will be the grateful one if you make a success of his play. Your parents will be very proud of you.'

Laurence shrugged. 'I don't think they will. They're living in hopes that I shall go back to the farm.'

Joanna said seriously, 'But you wouldn't be happy there, would you?'

He glanced quickly at her, and then away. 'I might some day, with the right kind of girl. Funny, that aspect of it never occurred to me before this moment.'

'What aspect?' she asked curiously.

Laurence dug his hands into his pockets and frowned down at the ground.

'Thinking in terms of settling down on a farm with the right girl. I'd always thought of settling down on my own. A life partner never entered into it.'

'But if you have a career on the stage it won't matter,' Joanna assured him lightly. 'Funny that you should think in terms of marriage when Candida is as well. You both came here burning with ambition to make your name in lights, yet now all you can hear is wedding bells. Why?'

Laurence grinned. 'It must be the climate plus the sea air. They say sea air improves your sexual appetite. Besides, with a woman it's different. They all want to get married some time in their lives.'

'Do you ... ?' Joanna paused, then rushed on, unable to stop. 'Do you think Candida will marry Ramón?' She had blushed like a rose, a habit she despaired of ever outgrowing, and lowered her lashes against hot cheeks.

Laurence said slowly, 'You mean do I think that Ramón will marry Candida, which isn't quite the same. He might. He certainly seems keen on her company.' He sensed her flinching. 'On the other hand, it might be just another affair to him, and like everything else he'll handle it admirably.'

Joanna gave a slight start as she felt his comforting grasp on her arm. Did he know of her love for Ramón? The question had popped out without her thinking, and some men were as intuitive as women where affairs of the heart were concerned. A swift glance at his profile did nothing to make her think that he had guessed, and she decided that he knew nothing.

CHAPTER EIGHT

PROMPTLY at eight o'clock that evening they all set out for the dinner party at Las Jacarandas. Candida had evidently gone to great pains to prepare for it. Her newly washed hair was like a spun gold and her evening dress had a flavour of Spain about it with the deep-flounced skirt and scooped neckline in Liberty silk in a soft multi-coloured print. There was no doubt about it, Candida was out to impress.

Laurence had raised a brow to murmur, '*Buenas tardes, señorita*,' and Nick had smiled. Joanna, sweet in pale pink brocade, sat in the back of Nick's big car with Laurence, and thought that the Villa Faustino could not be any more beautiful than Las Jacarandas. As they approached it the sun filtering through trees threw torchlike beams on the lush green garden which lay like a cultured diamond in the barbaric setting of the rocks. The wide heavy doorway was open to the villa, the interior was filled with flowers and guests arriving. Ramón stood waiting to welcome them, high, wide and handsome in evening dress. Joanna loved the sense of spacious elegance, the walls against which family portraits glowed, the strange mingling of simplicity and wealth, and everywhere flowers, their colour, their perfume invading shadowy corners.

The air was filled with the muted sounds of voices rising and falling and occasional light laughter as everyone was received by their host before drifting into a *salón* where waiters hovered with trays of drinks. Ramón's black head bent over Candida's hand and passed on to Joanna and they preceded the men into the *salón*.

There were about two dozen guests in all. With the exception of three business men and their wives, the other guests were all known to Nick and Joanna. There was an aroma of richness in the air, expensive cigars, exclusive perfume, expensive food and wine. The men were smart in white jackets, the ladies in model dresses as they stood chatting and drinking in small groups. The last of the guests arrived and Ramón came into the *salón* to mingle with them. With his usual speed and elegance, he seemed to be everywhere at once.

Joanna tried not to follow him around with her eyes, but he was like a magnet to her senses. It was the same in the dining room. He sat at the head of the table and she found herself looking across the glitter of silver and cut glass punctuated by exquisite flower arrangements to his dark face. Her heart told her he was easily the best-looking man in the room and the most exciting. Once she met his dark intent gaze and her heart fluttered, although she managed to lift her glass and smile. Of one thing she was certain—Ramón would never forget her, even if he did think back on her as a child. But it was no consolation to Joanna, who ached for his arms around her. In order to fight her need of him she assumed a bright exterior and chatted gaily to her father on one side and rather flirtatious cousin of Ramón's on the other.

Vicente del Dieldo was a banker in Tenerife. Joanna had met him several times at Ramón's parties. Like Ramón he was a bachelor, but he had brought young women with him on occasions. This evening he was alone and quite prepared to flirt with Joanna. Several times during dinner she caught Candida, who was seated opposite to her with Laurence, looking at her with amusement.

Laurence was not amused. His frown was frankly disapproving and Joanna wished it could have been Ramón. However, her host was engrossed with a near neighbour, a business associate whose pretty wife could not take her eyes off Ramón's lean tanned face. The familiar sound of voices rose and fell, punctuated by soft feminine laughter, the tinkling of cutlery accompanying the conversation.

'I have been to see Ramón's swimming pool at the Villa Faustino,' Vicente volunteered, studying Joanna's exquisite profile. 'I am considering having one installed at my villa in Tenerife.'

Joanna paused in the act of spooning up her gazpacho, a delicious chilled soup, and smiled at him. 'How nice. I've been in Ramón's. It's super,' she answered.

He raised a thick silky brow, for they were conversing in English, and said,

'Perhaps you would do me the honour of coming to sample mine when it is complete.'

'I might if I'm here. I'm going to London soon.'

'But you will be back.'

'I don't know.' Joanna was not interested in Vicente's swimming pool and she was beginning to see how dangerous it was to flirt with him. His veneer of charm was all that could be desired in courtesy and formality, but his dark eyes were conveying an unspoken message of admiration which was all the more potent for being unspoken. Joanna's sensitive perception felt it as something tangible, just as Ramón's presence acted like a drug on her senses. So she began to talk of trivialities and gave some of her attention to her father, seated on her other side. Although the food was excellent and served in just the right quantities—enough to enjoy each portion so as to enable one to wade through the endless courses without over-eating—to Joanna the evening seemed endless. Even the prospect of dancing later in the lovely ballroom failed to lift her spirits.

Vicente claimed her for the first three dances, elated, it seemed, by her obvious interest in him earlier on in the evening. Her naturalness and sweet air of sophistication fired his blood. Never before had he sensed such freshness combined in a quality of fragrant delicacy which Joanna possessed. There was no artifice about it. It was her natural self, as refreshing as spring water. When Laurence claimed her for the next dance, he sulkily relinquished his hold of her, only to come back later to claim her again and again.

She saw Ramón glide by with Candida in his arms and Laurence with several pretty girls, and she beginning to think that nothing short of being deliberately rude would free her from her unwanted partner when she was rescued and swung away from beneath Vicente's astonished nose. Long after Joanna remembered the beating of moths' wings in her throat accompanied by a tremendous feeling of relief. She was in Ramón's arms and was safe. But her joy was shortlived. Ramón was angry, very angry. He was speaking in a low voice, tightly controlled. Had she no conception of the spectacle she was making of herself with his cousin? If that was her way of making Laurence jealous, while he was sure it was successful, he did not think anything of it. Her father would no doubt be as disgusted as he was by her frivolous behaviour and would certainly not approve.

'But Ramón ...' she attempted on several occasions, and was instantly silenced.

'Excuses are not needed,' he broke in the first time. 'Such behaviour among my guests will be noted for future reference, and I will not have any friend of mine open to sly innuendoes now or at any time.'

'But Ramón ...' she tried again.

'If you care so much for this ... this English actor that you must resort to such behaviour in order to gain his favour, I will talk to him myself and ask him what his intentions are towards you.' He was talking very quickly, filling in the void as her voice died away, completely domiated by his angry growl. 'I find this present situation insupportable!'

'But, Ramón, you're being absurd,' Joanna said firmly, determined to have her say. 'I'm only doing with Vicente what you're doing with Candida. Or rather, Vicente is doing it with me, for to tell you the truth, I was getting a little scared of his ardour.'

'You must have given him some encouragement to behave as he did.'

Joanna moved her fingers in his grasp and his hand tightened on them cruelly.

'Ramón, you're hurting my hand!' she protested, but his grip only slackened slightly.

'It is nothing to what I would like to do to you,' he said, and she missed a step beneath his smouldering gaze. The next moment he had swung her out of the ballroom through open windows on to a terrace. He released her immediately and looked down on her coldly.

Joanna's eyes were now angry as well. 'At least Vicente doesn't treat me like a child!' she flared. 'And while we're on the subject of innuendoes, what about you and Candida?'

Ramón stiffened. His mouth thinned. 'That is my affair. It has nothing to do with you.'

His words were the equivalent of a slap in the face to Joanna. Her lips quivered. 'And my life has nothing to do with you either!' She spoke to his tie fearful lest he saw the tears brightening her eyes. As she turned to leave him he caught her wrist tightly.

'Anything you do in my house has. You will not dance with Vicente again this evening. Understand?'

Slowly she lifted her eyes to his face. The tears were forced back by her anger. It was cold and implacable. 'You might not be aware of it,' she said in level tones, 'But I've grown up in the last twelve months since I last saw Vicente. I am no longer a child, and he sees me as a woman. I'm grateful to him for that . . . I . . .'

Her wrist was released suddenly. Laurence had stepped on to the terrace with Candida who, walking up to Ramón, thrust her arm through his.

'Come along, Ramón. I wondered where you were and Laurence wants to dance with Joanna. We mustn't spoil their fun, you know.' Her voice, teasing and husky, grated on Joanna's ears, although she was grateful for the interruption. Instantly Ramón was once more his urbane and charming self.

He inclined his dark head. 'My apologies, Laurence. I trust you are enjoying the evening?'

'Very much,' Laurence replied, a hand on Joanna's arm. 'Shall we dance?' As they entered the ballroom, he asked, 'Is that Spanish chap who's monopolised you most of the evening an old flame of yours?'

'Vicente?' Joanna looked up at him as he steered her out among the dancers. 'Goodness, no! He's a cousin of Ramón's. I've known him for years.'

'From where I sat at dinner he seemed more than interested in you.'

Joanna was looking around the room and realised that Ramón was still on the terrace with Candida. She was only half listening to Laurence, but she answered him brightly enough.

'I think he's only just realised that I'm growing up. Ramón treats me like a child. Perhaps you've noticed?'

'Not particularly.' He swung her round from the path of an approaching couple and looked around the room. 'I can't see your admirer anywhere. He seems to have disappeared.'

'Vicente, you mean?' Joanna scanned the room and saw Ramón dancing now with Candida. The thought occurred to her that Ramón could have got rid of his cousin's unwelcome presence fairly quickly and she suddenly felt brighter. If Ramón did still think of her as a child at least he cared enough to look after her welfare. But it was small comfort when she saw his dark head bent down to listen to something Candida was saying. Suddenly she wanted to get away. 'Where's Daddy?' she asked. 'I haven't seen him since dinner.'

'Talking to one of the guests, a business associate of Ramón's, I fancy. Your father doesn't seem keen on dancing. Has he not ever thought of marrying again?' Laurence lifted a brow and looked down into Joanna's wide-eyed gaze.

'Daddy is a writer,' she answered rather sadly. 'He wouldn't have much time for a wife. His writing comes first with him.'

'Then he can't be much company for you. Don't you find it a little monotonous here? I mean, don't you want to have a good time?'

'You mean lots of boy-friends? I'm going back with you to London. I mean to have a good time, believe me.'

He laughed. 'You sound almost fierce! I hope that doesn't mean that you won't have much time for me. I'm very fond of you.' His grey eyes softened. 'In fact I'm more than fond. Do you mind?'

His expression was suddenly gentle and he saw the soft

response in her eyes, the pupils deepening, the gentle parting of her soft lips. 'Of course I don't mind. I'm fond of you too.'

As she went to bed Joanna thought again of Ramón dismissing his cousin so peremptorily from the villa. His reason for doing so had been, perhaps, unnecessarily exaggerated on her part, especially as Candida was humming to herself as she had gone to her room. The tune was evocative and underlain with triumph.

The high-powered car, arriving on time the following morning, gave Joanna a feeling of pride mingling with melancholy. Nothing had changed. She loved Ramón. The feeling was too real, too deep to be madness. Her whole being reacted to him, reached out to his. She felt the premonitory pain of loving adding to the pain of being unloved, and there was nothing she could do about it.

'*Buenos dias,* Juana. You slept well after the lateness of the hour last evening?' His dark eyes probed her face and travelled up to the mass of soft brown hair framing it. He looked vital and glowed with health, capable of tossing off lightly any number of late nights himself. 'You look fresh and sweet.'

He reached forward after opening the car door for her, and, taking her beach bag containing things she would need, he tossed it on to the back seat of the car.

'It was a good party, and everyone enjoyed it,' she said, slipping in beside him, and shaking back her hair. 'And I always sleep well.'

The road wound before them at speed, and they were both silent. Sometimes, as now, there was no necessity for conversation between them. She knew that Ramón was sensitive, and very receptive to the beauties of his island home which had become her own. It was something they shared along with the rather austere susceptibilities essential to his way of life. She wondered how Candida would react when she learned that on marriage to Ramón she would have little or no rights apart from her husband. Not only would her property become his to administer but she would also have to seek his permission to travel. What Candida's reactions would be Joanna could not say, and perhaps she would never know. Her heart ached for Ramón, although she knew he had sufficient strength and courage to deal with any situation which would arise in his marriage. One thing she had learned from him was to confront any embarrasing situation with dignity and tolerance. By the time they had reached the Villa Faustino, Joanna was perfectly cool and collected, determined to enjoy these short jaunts with the man she loved above all else.

During the hour that the Marquesa sat and Joanna worked time was very fleeting. Joanna worked, oblivious of her surroundings, with an intense concentration that was carrying her work forward to its final completion. It was only towards the end that she became aware of being hot and sticky, and thought longingly of the swimming pool with its cool, green depths below the surface, the shimmering radiance when the sun penetrated the water from which she finally emerged tingling fresh. This morning the Marquesa had fallen asleep sooner than usual, but Joanna painted on, entirely absorbed in her task.

How long Ramón had stood in the doorway watching her, she could not say. But gradually, with that inward reaction of her being to his presence, she turned her head slowly to see him leaning elegantly against the arched doorway, hands thrust into pockets, his extraordinary dark eyes fixed upon her. Wiser now to the way he had of making her pulses leap, Joanna willed herself to be calm.

With a swift glance at the sleeping Marquesa, she whispered, 'The portrait is nearly finished.'

He came forward at that to look at it. 'Wonderful,' he said on a slow smile of admiration. 'Clever girl!'

'You really like the portrait?' Ramón was walking with loose easy strides beside her on their way to the swimming pool, and she was looking up at him anxiously, so anxiously that she was not looking where she was going. The next moment she had tripped over a loose stone in her path and Ramón's arm shot out to encircle her waist. He released her as swiftly as he had caught her. 'You are as light as a breeze,' he said teasingly, and Joanna tried to borrow his coolness, knowing that she would not be able to withstand his nearness for much longer without betraying her own feelings. Joanna had known something like this would happen. Consequently her manner became a little withdrawn, and she only half listened to him expressing his satisfaction at the way she had done the portrait.

This morning he swam in the pool beside her and beat her easily in a race across its length in that maddening, lazy way of his, hinting at latent powerful strength beneath. When he sprang up on to the side of the pool and hauled her up beside him with a lean brown hand, he glanced down at her with a little flicker between his dark lashes.

'You left your dress further down,' he said casually. 'I will fetch it for you.'

Alone with him, Joanna knew it was dangerous to dwell upon his undoubted charms. Wistfully she watched him stride away, aware of rippling muscles, the smooth bronze of his skin, the long lazy stride and the crisp curling of his thick dark hair. His shoulders were strong and erect, his movements the easy ones of an athlete, a man who did everything well with his slumbering passions locked away, and waiting for the one woman to awaken them. Was that woman Candida? The thought was like a sword-thrust to her heart.

How long could she continue to treat him with ordinary friendship? It would not be easy, but harder still would be the knowledge that she would not see him at all when she left the island. If he married Candida it would be impossible for her to bear it, to bear his friendly visits to their villa and even play chess on occasions with Nick.

Would the pain lessen in time? At present Candida was a constant reminder in Ramón's absence, so the pain never let up. Joanna despaired. Somehow she put on a smile as he handed her the dress, went into the villa and came out without keeping him waiting long. He was there fresh and immaculate, and very dear, to take her arm with firm fingers and lead her to the car. The powerful car responded to the pressure of his foot, the touch of his firm brown hands on the wheel like a live thing. The beauty of the day caught at her heart. The sky had the luminosity of an opal with everything etched and clearly defined in the brilliant light.

Ramón seemed to have borrowed her silence, for he did not speak during the journey back. But just before they reached the Villa Rosario, he said,

'How long before you finish the portrait? I ask because it seems to me to be almost complete.'

A chill wind feathered across her skin although the air was still hot. He was anxious for the portrait to be finished, of course, because it would mean no more journeys to the Villa Faustino. From what she could gather he had been doing the quarterly returns for the estate and now that was nearing completion he wanted his day free again, free of escorting Joanna Main to do a portrait he had commissioned. Joanna felt that she was watching all hope and delusion of happiness vanishing from her life. She knew how much he meant to her, but not the enormity of it until now.

'I can finish it tomorrow if you wish,' she told him. 'If you're finding it inconvenient to take me, I can always drive there myself. I've told you that before.'

'So you did.' Was he laughing at her? Joanna was not sure. He was looking at her as he had done beside the swimming pool, his mouth amused, his dark eyes steady and intent. 'Are you still angry with me over last evening?'

Joanna started. She had completely forgotten it. 'No,' she answered truthfully. 'But I hate to think of Vicente having his evening spoiled because of me. There was no reason to send him away. If my behaviour embarrassed you, I'm sorry.'

He shrugged. 'And I apologise also. You were not to blame. I made no allowance for the fact that you are growing up and are no longer a child but a young woman. You possess an attractive naturalness combined with an air of elegant sophistication; an exciting blend sufficient to attract the male in no uncertain manner. If I am correct, you are now nineteen?' He tossed her a swift glance, taking in her fragile, brown-haired youthfulness, her sudden blush accentuating the piquancy of her face. 'A delightful age, and now you want to spread your wings.'

He swung the car on to the path leading to the Villa Rosario and the engine throbbed into silence. Slowly he turned to face her, looking down at her silently, his dark eyes intent. The air of critical aloofness which Joanna associated with the Marqués Ramón de Orleron y Faustino was again part of him. She tensed suddenly, tossing his compliments away on the chill wind that froze her beneath that impersonal regard. He was not interested in her as a woman. He looked as though he was disliking her growing up entirely. Even his compliments had been spoken with a maddening superiority. His wide shoulders shut out the light from the car window behind him and she clenched her hands on the seat. 'I'm almost twenty,' she said somewhat defiantly.

'So. We must do something about it.' He was out of the car and going round to open her door, virile and sunburned, his dark hair glinting with red lights in the sun. 'I shall call for you tomorrow morning as usual. *Adios*.'

His fingers left her arm as she straightened from the car and he strode round to his side of the car and slid inside. Not a word about Candida. He had not even stopped to see her. Joanna had never felt so shut out.

Candida followed her into her room. 'Had a nice morning?' she asked, smoking a cigarette and walking to the window to look out perhaps for a glimpse of Ramón's car. 'Ramón seemed to be in a hurry.'

Joanna put down her beach bag and looked at Candida's slim back. 'Yes, I had a good morning. Ramón probably has an appointment at Las Jacarandas. I suppose he has told you of his plans to have it done up?'

'Oh yes. As a matter of fact I've been helping him to choose new furnishings.' Candida turned slowly with a strange look on her face. 'Naturally he wants the place to look new to welcome his bride.'

Joanna drew in a breath sharply. A twinge, so acute as to be almost physical, shot through her. Her eyes, large and luminous, regarded her in rather a state of shock. 'You've told Daddy, of course?'

Candida lifted her mouth to blow out a long line of cigarette smoke ceilingward. 'Nick knows Las Jacarandas is being redecorated. He also knows that I shan't let him down as regards his play. My getting married won't interfere with it. I don't suppose we shall marry until Las Jacarandas is finished, and that won't be yet. As the play is due to open in the autumn we shall probably marry around Christmas.'

Candida was smiling warmly, but Joanna's heart was cold. The barrier between them was to her almost tangible. There was nothing in Candida's manner to suggest this. Her look, her voice, husky and vibrant, held nothing different. It's I who am not the same, Joanna thought miserably. Then quite suddenly she knew that behind Candida's smile was a sense of victory.

Slowly she took off her wrist watch and noted the time. 'I'll have to hurry or Rosita will be after me. She hates not serving lunch on time.' She began to unbutton her dress and Candida glided across the room as she added, 'If you're going downstairs, tell Rosita I won't be long.'

Candida paused at the door. 'As our engagement is not yet official, I can trust you to say nothing about it to anyone, can't I?' she said.

'I had no intention of telling anyone.' Joanna's voice was cold.

After lunch, Candida departed to her room and silence descended as Nick retired into his study to write. Laurence appropriated Joanna to work on the terrace painting the view.

'We will both do our own particular scene and compare,' he said, setting up the easels.

The afternoon slipped by with what seemed to Joanna amazing swiftness. Doing her favourite thing had ridded her of all tension and a sense of restlessness. The fascination of her favourite hobby had held her in thrall, leaving no time to think of problems on hand.

The arrival of Rosita with a tray containing afternoon coffee brought their work to a halt and each studied the other's efforts in silence.

'You really are good,' Joanna commented with her head on one side as she surveyed his easel. Rosita in the act of dispensing coffee added to her praise. But Laurence shook his head.

'I haven't the gift of fusing the colours as you have, Joanna,' he admitted, eyeing his picture critically. 'Your picture, for instance, lives and breathes. Mine doesn't.'

'Maybe you would do better with real life,' Rosita said, picking up her empty tray to depart.

Laurence grinned and stepped back to look Rosita over slowly. In her bright red dress, her skin swarthy, her black eyes luminously glowing, she made a colourful picture. His grin spread and he clicked his fingers.

'You're right, Rosita,' he cried. 'I'm going to paint you.'

'Oh no, you don't!' Rosita scuttled away as if a swarm of bees were after her and Laurence sank down into his chair, convulsed with laughing.

'It isn't a bad idea,' he said on a more sober note as he picked up his coffee. 'How's the picture of the Marquesa?'

'Almost finished.' Joanna, reluctant to talk about it, smiled with relief to see her father stroll on to the terrace. 'Coffee, Dad?' she asked.

'No, thanks.' Nick shook his head. 'What's the matter with Rosita? She's just zoomed past me on her way to the kitchen like the wind.'

He listened while they explained and examined their pictures drying on the easel. 'Rosita's right about painting real life. The women are fascinating creatures and very colourful in national dress. Incidentally, there's a good show on this evening in Las Palmas. Like to go?'

'Yes, Daddy, please. Are you going to take us?' Joanna smiled up at him as he leaned back against the terrace wall, her coffee forgotten. Action was what she craved, anything to take her mind from Candida and Ramón. Besides, in her opinion her father did not go out enough to enjoy himself.

She always enjoyed the run into Las Palmas. The journey through pine groves, tunnels and small villages was a colourful one. The island possessed a surfeit of water reflected in the lush growth of fruits including almonds and raisins, potatoes, maize, tomatoes, and bananas. The pines were particularly lovely amidst the grandeur of the mountains. Nick was a steady driver, preferring to enjoy the scenery and not cut corners.

Joanna felt that her father, like herself, revelled in the sultry atmosphere which clung together with the hot sun into numbing their faculties—pleasantly so. In some strange way she had thought that Nick had been rather reluctant to have his home life invaded by guests who were staying as long as Laurence and Candida. The Villa Rosario had been open as long as she could remember to artists and friends, but they had not been encouraged to stay long, not long enough to keep her father from his writing. Now he seemed to be enjoying it. He was relaxed, easy, free for the moment from the demands of his work, and she was happy to see him enjoying life. Ramón did not come so often to play chess since Candida had arrived. Once he was married, he would not come at all. Nick would miss him. So would she miss those evenings when she had partnered him herself if Nick had work to finish. Ramón had tutored her well, and their games together had been exciting and very enjoyable. With her eyes fixed in an enchanted stare on the chessboard every moment had been shared; a slow smile, a movement of the head, and they spoke volumes to each other. Now it was all over, or would be soon when Ramón announced his engagement to Candida.

They were entering the narrow cobbled streets of the town lined with houses of Spanish architecture with wooden carvings and small balconies, and on to the wider roads and the more exclusive locality. The entrance to the five-star hotel, well known for its smart clientele and sparkling floor shows, was approached by a wide sweep of a tree-lined drive off the esplanade. They parked the car and Nick went on ahead to book a table. He met them as they were entering the foyer.

'I'm sorry,' he said with a wry smile. 'I'm afraid they're booked up.'

Laurence shrugged goodhumouredly. 'Hard luck. Can't we go somewhere else?'

Nick did not answer. He was watching a couple about to enter the hotel, a striking couple, the man dark and handsome, the woman blonde and lovely.

Nick smiled. 'We're in luck. Here's Ramón and Candida.'

'But we can't butt in, Daddy . . .' Joanna began. The sudden appearance of Ramón had made her feel strangely numb. It was like a pain-killing drug that would eventually wear off and leave a pain far worse than the one before.

Ramón was smiling, his teeth a bar of whiteness in his tanned face, as he came forward with Candida. 'This is indeed a surprise,' he said. 'I had no idea you were coming here.'

'We aren't,' said Nick. 'We can't get a table.'

'Then I insist upon you sharing ours,' Ramón answered without hesitation.

Nick hesitated. 'Sure we shan't be butting in?' He smiled and made a gesture of apology. 'Sorry, Ramón. Sure we're not intruding?'

Ramón's frown cleared as he comprehended. 'You are my friends. It will give me great pleasure to accept your company for the evening.' He took Candida's arm and Joanna's, debonair and charming, and led the way into the hotel. Joanna guessed that he used the hotel for private and business reasons, and his table was probably permanently booked. He seated Candida while Laurence drew out a chair for Joanna and the waiters scuttled off to provide more chairs for them. In an effort to withstand her unhappiness, Joanna smiled and managed to look as if she was enjoying herself.

The food was excellent, the wine a rich vintage, and it helped. But Joanna's throat was so constricted most of the time that it surprised her how she managed to swallow it. The conversation was varied. Nick was encouraged to talk about his play, and the subject of chess came up when Ramón remarked that there was a contest on at Tenerife with the leading expert chess players taking part. He smiled across the table with mockery and amusement at Joanna as he mentioned it, and her heart closed into a tight cold ball, knowing that those precious intimate hours they had shared over the chessboard meant little or nothing to him.

The men lighted cigars, with Ramón flicking on a silver lighter to ignite Candida's cigarette before following suit with the men. The floor show began. It had a continental flavour; an American couple, uproariously funny, an Italian singer, handsome and moving, a Spanish juggler, slim-hipped, charming and agile, and the star turn of the evening, a beautiful Spanish dancer. When the juggler appeared he announced regretfully that his pretty girl assistant could not be there that evening, and he would like to choose one from the audience. His dark eyes roamed the tables and he stepped out of the limelight to make a polite bow to Joanna. But before he could state his request, Ramón was whispering urgently to Candida, who rose to her feet. The juggler bowed to Ramón's whispered Spanish and escorted Candida to the spotlight as the people applauded. Joanna froze in her chair. How dared he? Still treating her like a child! Or had he thought she was not capable of assisting in the act? Candida, of course, was as much at home in the limelight as sitting there at the table. It had all happened so quickly and Ramón had handled the situation so well that few people guessed that the juggler had been fobbed off with the one he did not choose.

Nick had raised a brow and tapped the ash from his cigar, Laurence had looked rather perplexed, then carried on his conversation with Nick. And now Ramón was leaning across the table to Joanna.

'Candida is accustomed to facing an audience,' he said. 'Had anything gone wrong it could have spoiled your evening and ...' He broke off abruptly and the dark eyes searched her set face. 'You are not angry, Juana?'

Joanna forced herself to be polite, bearing in mind that she was his guest. She did her best, but her voice was cold, her eyes bleak. 'Why must you always insist upon treating me as a child?' she demanded in a low undertone spoken under the cover of conversation between Nick and Laurence. 'Surely children, if you regard me as one, are natural actors. I'm sure I would have done as well as Candida.'

The beginning of the act put an end to further conversation and it passed smoothly. The spotlight shone on Candida's golden hair as she carried out her duties, winning vociferous applause at the end. The Spanish dancer came into the circle of light as though borne on a breeze. The brilliant scarlet flounces of her skirt were piped with white and the tight satin bodice revealed the lovely lines of her bust. Her hair cascaded down rich, black and glossy, on to her bare beautiful shoulders, fastened back over one small ear by a red hibiscus. Her dark luminous eyes flashed and her body moved to the rattle of castanets which she held in her hand. The pale rose light drenching her deepened to crimson, then, gold as the dance became faster and faster. The gaze of the audience was drawn to her swirling figure as a moth to a flame and there was a faint sigh of rapture as the dance ended and the dancer was curtseying to the applause.

The lights went up to dancing, and guests moved on to the floor. Ramón escorted Candida and Laurence partnered Joanna. Nick was content to smoke his cigar and watch. Dancing was not in his line, although he knew it was one of the required social graces. His eyes were thoughtful as he watched Joanna and Laurence and he looked vulnerable and worried. So thought Joanna, who caught his eye as she circled the room in Laurence's arms, and her smile was reassuring and warm. His look had gone straight to her heart, for she had seen in it all the love she had craved from him since her mother had died. It had been there all the time even though he had not shown it.

The lighting was softly muted like the orchestra with its sonorous beat. Beautifully dressed sunburned people gave themselves to the pleasure of the dance and the floor was filled with moving figures. Uncertain what to wear, Joanna had decided upon a cream cotton dress embroidered around the neck and skirt in multi-coloured silks. The neck was drawn up with a silken cord and could be worn off the shoulders. Tonight she wore it that way, showing the tender curve of her neck and shoulders, honey gold and alluring. There was an untouched air about her which presented a picture of extreme youth with a provocative touch of elegance.

Candida wore a blue poncho in Chinese figured silk with a white fringe over a blue skirt. It was a trifle exotic and suited her blonde beauty. Everyone in the room probably admired it when she was in the spotlight assisting the juggler in his act. Ramón obviously admired it too. His head was inclined down to her upturned face as he swung her by among the dancers, and Joanna looked quickly away. It was inevitable that Ramón would ask her for a dance sooner or later, and it was also inevitable that she would succumb to his charm. Oblivious of Candida watching them glide away, Joanna, held correctly in Ramón's strong arms, danced as if in a dream. It was a dream from which she never wanted to wake. Her heart thudded with the primitive beat of the drums, her will was powerless, her body melting into his. She felt him draw her closer when they entered a congested part of the room in a silence more powerful than words. Her eyes wandered up to the firm chin and well cut lips, and she was tormented with an aching longing to feel his mouth against hers.

It was shattering to think that he and Candida had reached an agreement. Knowing Ramón, Joanna knew he would put Nick's play first. Secure in the knowledge that Candida loved him, he was content to wait until the play was on the way to success before announcing anything. She was aware of Ramón speaking above her ear.

'Are you still angry with me?' he asked softly.

Joanna lowered her head and kept back the tears, recalling the many years of shared life, shared laughter they had enjoyed together. Angry with him? How could she be when she loved him more than life?

'Why did you do it?' she whispered. 'It would have been

a new experience for me, and he was a very attractive young man.'

'Ah, but you must admit that Candida played her part professionally,' he teased.

'And you mean I wouldn't? After all, he did choose me.' She lifted her head to look up at him accusingly.

'And you wanted to impress Laurence. You underrate your charms. There is no necessity to impress him. You know what I think . . .'

'I don't want to know what you think, Ramón,' she told him fiercely. Let him think that she was in love with Laurence! It would save her pride. She swallowed on a dry throat and added, 'I only want you to leave me alone. I'm quite capable of running my own life, and I do have a father.'

She knew she had hurt him. He was proud, and would not venture to seek another reproof. Well, what did she care? But she did.

His fingers tightened on hers. His hand on her back seemed to squeeze her heart. His tones without emotion, Ramón said, 'Why is it necessary for us to quarrel each time we meet socially? You have changed, Juana, since this Englishman appeared. I would not say that you have grown up more, for you have the touchiness of the very young. You have not learned restraint. You do not control your emotions. You explode too easily.'

The dance number was nearing the end and Joanna almost tore herself free of his arms. 'If I have changed then all I can say is that it's a pity you haven't! You still insist on running my life for me when I don't want you to,' she burst out feelingly.

'You mean you don't want me in your life?'

'Of course I do. But not as a guardian. Why won't you treat me as you do Candida? As a woman? Then perhaps I might begin to behave like one.'

The band chose that moment to fade into silence and they stood eyeing each other like contestants. Ramón's arms slid to his sides and he said slowly, 'I have known you much longer than I have known Candida. I was right, you have changed. What I feel for you cannot in the widest sense compare with what I feel for Candida.' He held out a hand to restrain her as she was about to walk back to their table. 'Has our friendship meant so little to you?'

Cold as a statue and as stiff, Joanna raised her eyes to his. 'Yes. It has meant living in a sheltered world, not a real one but one from which I had to emerge some day and meet life like anyone else. I can't blame you for keeping up the illusion and treating me like a child. Daddy is still apt to do the same.' She smiled, but it was a smile that did not reach her eyes. 'Perhaps what I need is a complete break from here. Perhaps going to London is a good idea after all.'

She walked back to their table, her head held high. I ought to cry, she thought, but some hurt went beyond tears. Her whole being felt numb with only her legs capable of movement, and they began to tremble as she sat down. She never did remember much about the rest of that evening, except that it was about the worst one in her life.

CHAPTER NINE

JOANNA awoke the next morning to think with mixed feelings about her usual morning visit to the Villa Faustino. Ramón would be with her for most of the time. There would be no avoiding him. Their friendship now had no meaning. What it had meant to him, she would never know. Not much, since he had given her to understand it was nowhere near the quality of what he felt for Candida. What a good thing it was that he would never know what a fool she had been over him! She would leave the island with her secret intact. He would never know. Leaving the island would tear her heart in two, but the pain would grow less in time—it had to. Would she ever come back? Could it be the beginning of a new life?

She would miss her painting, the mountain flowers, the banana plantations, her friends, the warm greetings of her neighbours, the loving care of Rosita and her jaunts to the docks in Las Palmas to fetch the mail when something important was expected. There would be no more mornings like this morning, standing at her window breathing in the crystal clear air and gazing at the glittering outline of the mountains against the sky. An awful sense of desolation hung over her like a cloud. She could not recognise herself as the girl who had gone about so gaily in her waking hours to sleep dreamlessly at night. She had gazed across at Las Jacarandas with dreams in her eyes because it meant Ramón, who had been her very dear friend. Now that friendship had ended. Nothing could come of it except heartbreak for herself. Joanna lifted her chin militantly. She might have lost her own self-assurance, but it was coming back.

She turned impulsively to her wardrobe and selected a delicate lilac gingham foursome—over-shirt, minute shorts, bikini and bra. She brushed her hair after a perfumed bath which made her smell delicious, and tied a bond of the lilac gingham round her head to hang down over one shoulder. Then she went down to breakfast. Rosita's admiring glance at her outfit gave her confidence, but her fingers trembled as she lifted her fruit juice. She was dreading Ramón's arrival. He had not attempted to stop her from walking back to their table the previous evening after their sharp exchange of words on the dance floor. He was not Ramón any longer. He was the Marqués de Orleron y Faustino. He would no longer treat her with the affection she had known. He would take her at her word.

Candida had not put in an appearance when the big car drew up, its shining wings close to the herbaceous border of the path. Again Joanna lifted her chin and went gaily to meet him. Her long, honey-gold legs twinkling in the sun, her slender neck supporting her piquant face like a flower.

At the car she paused for resentment at her appearance, but Ramón's reaction was merely the lifting of a silky brow as he swung open the car door for her to slide inside. He had greeted her politely in Spanish and she had returned his serve with equal politeness. Then his firm brown hands, edged by immaculate cuffs, had taken the wheel of the car and they slid away.

'I suppose this is our last day at the Villa Faustino,' she said in her frank forthright way.

'And why should it be our last day?'

His swift intent glance prompted her to add, 'The portrait is almost finished. You said yourself . . .'

'I was inquiring about it for a reason. In any case, I do not expect you to break off your friendship with my *abuela* when the portrait is completed. She has become dependent to a certain extent on your visits. You are a young woman of sensibility who would not willingly cause distress to anyone. You would cause it to *Abuela* should your visits to her cease.'

Joanna bit in her soft lip. 'I am fond of the Marquesa, very fond. I think she's sweet and I've enjoyed my visits very much. But you have work of your own to do . . . the improvements at Las Jacarandas, for example. You must be in a hurry to complete it. It . . . it's most important to you.'

'But *Abuela* is very much more important to me.'

At the moment, thought Joanna, clasping her hands tightly together in her lap. But wait until you marry Candida. She'll insist on coming first. But I love you for putting human relations before possessions.

Aloud, she said soberly, 'The Marquesa is important to me too. All my friends are.' She stole a glance at his beloved profile and added, 'Material possessions aren't that important.'

'I agree. Have you reached that conclusion in regard to Laurence? I believe he is as yet an unknown actor,' he said dryly.

'No, I have not, and yes, he is, in that order,' she answered promptly. Imperceptibly the tension in her eased. 'I wouldn't say that money is the most important thing in marriage—not here on the island anyway. What could be more comfortable than the caves in the hills if you fancy a caveman?'

Ramón flicked a startled glance in her direction. 'You do not mean you are . . . er . . . interested in one of the cave-dwellers?'

Joanna laughed. 'I was teasing.'

'Then please continue with your nonsense, for it means we are friends again.' He was smiling.

'Then we are friends,' she conceded lightly.

Life would be easier that way, she told herself. It was necessary to keep things on a certain level in order not to get out of one's depth. The day seemed suddenly to be one of breathtaking beauty. The sky was a vast ceiling of blue with the mountains rising majestically against it. As they travelled along the hot dusty road visions of a cool swimming pool came to mind.

'Are you having a swimming pool at Las Jacarandas?' she asked conversationally.

'You must come and see for yourself when the work is done,' he answered laconically. His words brought an ache of longing for she knew she would be in London before then. She fell into silence and there was no sound save the hum of the car and the sound of the faint breeze among the trees.

They sat together, yet Joanna knew they could not have been further apart. Even so, it was not possible to be unaware of him. His clear-cut profile, the faint emanation of masculine fragrance from good grooming when he stirred beside her, her hunger for his arms around her, were moving her profoundly. At the thought of Candida in his home, sharing his life, the blood beat in her temples to bring on an aching head—she who had never know what it was to have a headache in her life.

They were descending now to sweep out on to the main highway joining the flow of traffic to Las Palmas. Joanna closed her eyes. Impossible to contemplate life without him, she thought, never again to see that intent look which masked some hidden power from within. He would no longer share an evening with Nick and herself as he used to; to talk, play chess or listen lazily with that deceptive nonchalance masking vitality that highlighted his every mannerism.

Opening her eyes slowly, she turned to gaze through the window. What she saw shook her out of her unhappy reverie. 'You've missed the road leading to the Villa Faustino,' she cried urgently, placing a hand on his arm. 'You're going straight on.'

'We are not going to the Villa Faustino this morning,' he announced calmly. 'We are going on to Las Palmas. I have business there.'

Her eyes widened. 'But ... but won't the Marquesa be expecting us?' she cried, wondering at the sudden change of plan.

'I told Abuela yesterday that we would not be going to the villa this morning.'

'You mean we're going this afternoon?'

'No. There is *mañana* and all the *mañanas*,' was the suave reply. He went on. 'No doubt you are wondering why I brought you along. I have a particular reason for doing so. First I have a call to make at the docks concerning a shipment of materials for alterations at Las Jacarandas.

Then I need your help in choosing a present, a rather important one for a lady friend, a special lady friend.' He turned to smile at her charmingly with the old warmth. 'You will do that for me?'

Something froze inside Joanna, but she nodded and managed a smile.

'Do I know the lady?' she asked.

'You know her,' he replied. That was all.

The ship from South Africa was already in dock when they arrived on the harbour. She lay at anchor and a steady stream of passengers was coming ashore down the gangway. The quay swarmed with taxi drivers, vendors of goods and friends of the people arriving. They were a mixed bag of English, American and South Africans showing a surfeit of tanned limbs in shorts and flowered dresses. Ramón left the car to leap up the gangway with the ease of an athlete with the sun glinting on his thick dark hair.

Joanna watched with interest as Ramón disappeared on board and imagined herself sailing to England. Only the idea did not enchant her any more. What had once been her favourite dream was now more of a nightmare when she realised it would be like sailing out of Ramón's life. She felt sad and dispirited, unequal to rising and dealing with him as lightheartedly as she knew she had to if he was not to guess her secret. But there was a yearning though painful sweetness in having him slide into the car again beside her after putting a heap of parcels in the boot of the car with the help of one of the ship's stewards. Then he was looking straight into her eyes, his own dark and intent.

His voice was level, assured. 'That did not take long, did it? And now we will go for a cool drink before doing our shopping.'

He started the car and they left the harbour to make their way to the town. As a rule Joanna was not too fond of Las Palmas itself, with the shops crammed full of gifts for tourists who came ashore when the big liners pulled in for refuelling. She had always found it too commercial. But this morning with the sun breaking through a pearly sky, the picturesque palm trees silhouetted against the blue and the dazzle of white buildings festooned with window boxes of brilliant hue, there was a kind of aching beauty about it.

He parked the car and led her to an outdoor café, an unpretentious little place gay with striped awnings and little umbrella-topped tables where he ordered iced drinks. His touch on her arm, light though it had been, had set unknown fires alight inside her. Friendly affection, she was discovering, was harder to fight than total indifference. The lightest touch from Ramón and her love for him spilled over. He was behaving as though they had never quarrelled, as though Candida did not exist.

The waiter put down their drinks in tall glasses. Joanna raised hers and he did likewise. Then she had to lower her eyes. In the clear light his features were handsomely well-defined, his smooth brown skin flatteringly darker.

He was so dear. Joanna knew fleetingly that had he made it clear beforehand that they were not going to the Villa Faustino that morning, she would not have come to Las Palmas with him. Continuing their acquaintance was not going to help to rid herself of her obsession for him—for that was what it was, an obsession which gave her no peace. The iced drink went slowly down her parched throat, the coolness steadying her nerves. What if thoughts of Candida did cloud the beauty of the morning? She was here with Ramón in what was to her the most beautiful place in the world.

They lingered over their drink, friendly yet withdrawn. Joanna refused a second one and prepared herself for the familiar feeling of his fingers on her elbow as he led her to the shops. The many gift shops with their cheap ware were ignored in favour of the more expensive establishments. Ramón's taste in presents was impeccable, and in the plush atmosphere of goods elegantly displayed on stands, he was immediately recognised by the head of the department, who came forward to greet him like royalty.

Upon Ramón requesting the music department the red carpet was metaphorically rolled out for them, with the manager leading the way. Among the selection of expensive record players and stereo equipment, Ramón turned to look down at Joanna standing silently by his side. The manager stood a little distance away, also smiling at Joanna with a look of undisguised admiration. In the lilac sun-suit her golden limbs were enchanting. If Ramón noticed the man's absorption in her he ignored it. His voice was kind and free from satire.

'This lady friend of mine is young enough to enjoy the latest music,' he said. 'Perhaps you would help me to choose. Most young people like music. I thought a record player, stereo equipment and records. What do you say?'

Joanna smiled, 'Sounds fabulous!'

In the matter of choosing, money was no object, and she became absorbed in her task, mindful of choosing a gift she would enjoy, and also one which would meet with his approval. Ramón added his own choice to the mounting pile of records accompanying the gift, and Joanna moved away while he signed a cheque, extracted a note from his wallet to be sent with the gift, and gave the address for it to be delivered. It was to be sent to the Villa Rosario.

'And now,' said Ramón, 'we will go to lunch.'

Joanna made no reply but managed a smile as he held the car door open for her to slide into her seat. She had never felt less like eating. She felt too strung up and horribly alone. Somehow she had known that the gift was for Candida, yet she had refused to face it until he had given the address. Joanna had never felt so wretched in her life. Lucky Candida, she thought, to be loved and needed by Ramón; to feel the strength of his arms around her; to know that she was adored, protected and loved.

The car was now sweeping off the esplanade to glide up to the entrance of the hotel they had visited the previous evening. Joanna's spirits sank lower as she recalled the sharp words they had exchanged there on the dance floor. But Ramón apparently did not share her aversion to the place, and helped her from the car to stroll with a loose-limbed elegance beside her. Joanna hoped that Ramón had booked some unobtrusive corner table where she could relax in a chair that was comfortable and not think back too longingly on the swimming pool at the Villa Faustino. They were met at the door of the dining room by one of the vast number of white-jacketed waiters who seemed continually to move between the immaculate tables, which were set well spaced in order for the diners to look out of picture windows on to lawns where palms and flowers were sprinkled with the brilliance of the sun. Beyond lay the sparkling sea dotted with yachts and colourful boats.

Joanna was aware, as if from a distance, of the chattering and laughter, the clinking of glasses and dishes, and her throat felt dry as if she had been chain smoking, a thing she had never done.

'You do not mind coming here?' Ramón had seated her and dropped into his chair opposite, looking negligent and part of the select clientele. 'This is my favourite haunt when I am in Las Palmas and I wanted it to be yours also!'

Joanna was not a coward and she did not shirk the unpleasant. 'You mean our little disagreement of last evening? I can hardly see it affecting my liking for the place. After all, the prices here are way beyond my purse, so I shall have to make the most of it while I'm here.'

The flippant note in her voice made him darken beneath his tan. His eyes narrowed into dark points and he said forcefully, 'I have never heard you speak like this before. You have always been so refreshingly free and young in your outlook. There is no question of different standards between you and me, never has been. Why do they begin now?'

It was impossible to ignore his sudden anger. It was coming across the table to her in waves. There was silence while the waiter brought them wine and Ramón conferred over the order. He knew her favourite dishes, which mostly were his own, and he ordered accordingly. Then the head waiter was pouring out the wine and waiting for their approval as they sipped it. Then he had gone. The small interruption had gone a long way to helping Joanna to quiet her emotions.

'I'm sorry. I didn't mean to offend,' she admitted miserably.

He said curtly with so softening of his expression, 'Let it pass.'

Her overwrought mind interrupted his offhand manner as one of boredom. She babbled, unable to stop the flow of words, 'But I can't let it pass, Ramón. You treat me like ... like an uncle taking his niece out for a treat. I'm too young to differentiate and too old for toys. I'm grown up. Lots of girls are married at my age. Some, even Spanish girls, are receiving suitors. You make me so mad I ...'

'Be quiet and remember where you are,' he rapped out furiously. 'You might be growing up, but you are certainly behaving like a child at this moment. I have no idea what has got into you. If you have some grievance against me then tell me about it. But not in a public place for all to hear.'

He had kept his voice down and his nostrils had thinned slightly as he had leaned across the table. Joanna had bent her head to hide her working mouth, and to keep the tears at bay.

His next words dropped like pebbles in the pool of her misery. 'What is it you want of me?' His eyes searched her face, willing her to look at him. 'Do you want me to talk to your father on Laurence's behalf? Is the man worth upsetting yourself over? Would it not be wiser for you to go to London before making your mind up about any man?'

Joanna tightened her fingers around her empty glass. Slowly she lifted her eyes, to find him much too close. The irises of his dark eyes were black with anger, his firm lips tight. She leaned back in her chair, unable to withstand his intent look, and looked down at her glass.

'Thanks for the advice,' she answered in a low voice. 'I'm sorry for what I said just now. I had no right to say such things.'

'No. You had not.' Ramón sat back in his chair and looked at her. His dark eyes glittered cold as stones. 'Shall we leave it at that?'

The waiter came with the first course and the meal commenced. Fortunately the place was filled with an interesting clientele and Joanna was able to gaze either at the diners or through the window at the superb view. The gardens were looking particularly lovely, and with an ache in her heart, Joanna was sure that she had never seen such beauty of growth as there was this summer. Trees were laden down with thick foliage and blossoms spilled in great profusion from countless bushes. But the beauty of her surroundings only seemed to add weight to the heaviness of her heart.

Later when Ramón was delivering her at her door he broke the silence that had followed them all the way back from Las Palmas. During that very swift run back to the Villa Rosario, Joanna had an odd idea that he had completely forgotten her presence at his side; that when she stepped from the car, he would scarcely notice that she had gone.

'When I call for you tomorrow I would appreciate it if you would wear something more suited to *Abuela's* taste. I am not speaking disparagingly about your sun-dress. Indeed, I would say it is deliciously seductive.' Here a smile twinkled somewhat reluctantly in the dark eyes. 'But you understand?'

He stood looking down at the delicate colour rising in her face, having come round to her side of the car to help her out. His wide shoulders shut out the sun's glare. He was right, of course—she was too fond of his grandmother to want to distress her in any way. His politeness was a mixture of relief and pain. He was being subtle and nice too. She felt suddenly ashamed of her behaviour.

'I'm sorry,' she said, looking somewhere in the region of his tie. 'It was wrong of me to put it on. But it was so warm in the *salón* when I was working.'

He inclined his dark head. Amusement coloured his voice. 'I think it was an oversight. For the moment you forgot that you are now a young lady, a *señorita* whom my *abuela* will expect to behave with decorum.' His tone was now openly mocking. 'Do not distress yourself. Growing up will have its drawbacks, but it will also have its compensations. *Adios* until tomorrow.'

Did his lips touch her hair above the gingham band on

her head? Joanna could not have sworn to it. But she did know that had she been any other woman he would never have asked what she required of him. He would have known as a man who was experienced with women. It was clear that she held no attraction for him as a woman. She had been foolish to allow her love for him to dictate her emotions and actions. From now on she would be different and really grow up by concealing her feelings beneath a bright exterior.

Ramón's car had hardly left the villa than Joanna was alerted to a small van drawing up at the door. In utter surprise she read the name on it and waited in the doorway while a young man got out with several parcels.

The shop had certainly lost no time in delivering them since Ramón had ordered them, she thought, and wondered if Candida was around.

'Señorita Joanna Main?' the young man asked, stopping in front of her with a lifted brow, his dark eyes full of appraisal at her slender form.

She nodded dazedly and stepped aside for him to take the parcels into the hall where he deposited them on a table. He had been gone some time before she dared to pick up the note attached. At last, opening it with shaking fingers, she saw Ramón's monogram at the top of the sheet of notepaper and read the message beneath. It was written in his masculine hand and read:

'Since you refused to accept payment for the portrait which you so kindly painted I venture to hope that you will accept this small present as a token of my gratitude and sincere thanks. Ramón.'

Joanna was shattered. So the present had been for her! What had he said? A rather important present for a special lady friend. Herself. Joanna's hands flew to her hot cheeks in dismay. And she thought it was for Candida! A small present, he called it. With shaking fingers she unwrapped stereo equipment, a record player and records worth hundreds of pounds. He had referred to her as a special lady friend and she had accused him of treating her like a child! She stood hands outstretched palms downward, pressing hard on the table as she tried to take it all in.

How foolish she had been to underestimate Ramón's intelligence! Of course he had been aware of her growing up, but he had not looked on her with changed eyes. To him she was little Joanna Main, his very dear friend, and not to be confused with his women friends who made him feel very much a man. She, Joanna Main, would never count with him in any other way than that of a dear friend. His bones would never melt at her approach, nor his heartbeats quicken as hers did at the sight of him. He cared for his other friends as much as he cared for her. That was how she had to regard him in the future, as a friend. Joanna went slowly up to her room, leaving the gift Ramón had bought for her on the hall table. By the time she went downstairs again, Rosita would have seen it, unwrapped it and taken it into the lounge. Normally the gift would have delighted her. Now she could not care less if she never saw it again.

The others were on the terrace when Joanna went downstairs some time later. Apparently they had just returned from Nick's study where they had gone to finish the morning's work right after lunch. Now they all relaxed over an iced drink. The air was still, the sun hot, and nothing stirred in the garden except the occasional small bird with its bright wings flashing colourfully as it swooped from tree to tree.

'Hello,' said Nick, blowing smoke lazily from his cigarette and looking fondly at his daughter. 'Rosita says you have had a stereo and lots of records from Ramón. Cost quite a packet.'

Joanna sat down at the small table and said casually, 'A gift for painting the portrait of the Marquesa. I refused payment, and Ramón insisted upon a gift.'

'But he's rolling in money,' Laurence exclaimed beside her. 'He wouldn't have missed whatever he paid you.'

Joanna poured out a glass of iced lemonade from a jug on the table.

'I couldn't accept payment from Ramón for a favour. I've

known him practically all my life,' she answered, and picked up her glass.

'Like a brother,' murmured Candida cryptically. Like Joanna, she was wearing a sleeveless camisole top and jeans. Unlike Joanna's which were a pale blue and very much laundered, Candida's were buttercup yellow and gave her a golden look from the top of her shining hair to her bare feet. She was smoking a cigarette and had flung back her head to exhale a line of smoke from pursed red lips showing the long, lovely line of her throat.

Joanna thought, she looks so sure of herself and of Ramón, and was thankful that she had decided to put on her sunglasses. They acted as a shield against Candida's worldliness, against which she always felt naïve and defenceless. Behind her sunglasses she had more confidence, and was more able to present a cool front. Candida was clearly jolted and not a little jealous of Ramón's expensive gift. Slowly she had turned her head to look derisively at Joanna; an assured, ambitious young woman out for a career plus a man; or so it seemed. The cold blue eyes slid over her boyish figure, her slim arms enriched with a deep peach tan which highlighted the clearness of her eyes, the healthy pink of her lips presenting an enchanting picture of youth combined with a promise of future elegance.

'Your Joanna is growing up fast, Nick,' she observed. 'She is learning that next to money, expensive gifts are a girl's best friends.'

'Eh now, I'm not having that,' Laurence cut in lazily. 'I reckon Ramón has a bargain there. Any portrait of Joanna's, to my way of thinking, is of far more value than this present she has received.' He looked at Nick. 'If you're going to be busy this afternoon I'll go with Joanna to try out this present of hers. Want to come, Candida?' He grinned amiably. 'They say that music calms the savage breast. I dare say that even you are not immune to that.'

Surprisingly, Candida did not take offence but stubbed out her cigarette and rose to her feet with sensual feminine movements. And Joanna, to whom any kind of movement was essential in her present mood, felt almost happy as

Laurence armed her and Candida from the terrace.

In the lounge Joanna began to relax. Together they went through the records, exclaiming with pleasure at their own particular favourites. Laurence took charge, handling the expensive equipment with a punctiliousness almost reverent, as though he was aware of what the gift meant to Joanna. Joanna could not help but be aware of this, and she felt herself warming towards him. He had taken her side against Candida and almost imperceptibly her feeling for him increased. It might not be so difficult to drift into a deeper relationship with him. From what she could gather both he and Candida represented another world; a world where one fostered one's own independence. It was an alien world to the one in which she had been brought up with a different sense of values.

Here on the island life was vastly different. Ramón strode through it like a king; his brilliance, his virile masculinity and charm; his dynamic personality making him a law unto himself. Yet without him she knew that the island would be barren to her despite its beauty. Once away from the island it was just possible that she might forget him; learn to accept a different way of life. It was surprising how the thought comforted, surprising how coolly she could watch Candida leave the lounge later to go to prepare herself for an evening out with Ramón.

CHAPTER TEN

JOANNA spared some thought on what to wear for her last visit to the Villa Faustino. With the feeling that sackcloth and ashes would be the right attire as she recalled how she had misjudged him, she put on a white spotted red print dress cut on Spanish lines with a frill around the skirt and the scooped-out neckline. With it she wore a chunky necklace and a matching bracelet and trod into white sandals.

The weather had changed during the night and it was considerably cooler this morning with the promise of rain later. Rosita followed her on to the terrace with the breakfast tray.

'You are looking very pretty this morning,' she remarked with a look of appraisal at the shining brown hair and lissom figure in the enchanting dress. 'Sometimes I think you are more Spanish than English.'

'The dress,' vouchsafed Joanna laconically. 'I'm finishing the portrait today, so this is the last time that I shall go to the Villa Faustino so early.'

Rosita paused in setting the table from her tray to give her a strange look. 'Maybe you will have something to tell me when you come back. *Si?*'

'What is there to tell?'

Rosita's grunt was more of a snort. 'Have it your own way. You will learn.'

'What shall I learn?' Joanna picked up her fruit juice, watched Rosita pick up the empty tray and turn to gaze out across the terrace at the view. The low clouds were casting dark green shadows across the banana plantations and the white dwellings stood out starkly on the mountain greenery. The sea beyond was placid, as still as Rosita, who was not looking at the view. Her gaze was directed a little to her right, and Joanna, following that gaze, saw that she was looking at Las Jacarandas.

The next moment Rosita had gone, leaving Joanna wishing that the morning was over. Somewhere out there Ramón would be already on his way to pick her up for the last time. She forced herself to eat a little, but it was hard work because her throat felt constricted, and she drank the coffee thirstily. It was no use trying to bolster up her morale for when Ramón arrived. She knew from past experience that it would disintegrate the moment he appeared. Her love for him, which had held a radiance rivalling that of the sun, moon and stars all together, was slowly and surely giving way to a painful and permanent ache. She still wanted so much to belong to him; to wake up in the morning and find him beside her; to have his children; to share his life and not the unsatisfying hours of friendship in his company.

As usual his arrival caught her unawares. The big car slid to a halt in all its dazzling sleekness as the sun slipped from behind a cloud with sudden brilliance. Picking up her beach bag, Joanna felt her heart begin to beat suffocatingly, and forcing strength into her legs she went to meet him. Once in the roomy car with her shoulders settled back comfortably against the soft leather, the trembling in her legs subsided. And now, she thought, to apologise. Ramón slanted her an interested glance as he slid in beside her.

'I like the dress,' he said, and smiled.

She looked up into his fine bronze face, at the thick black hair, and the long black eyelashes highlighted by the sun. Then she lowered her eyes to his hand about to start the car.

'Thanks,' she answered. Then, 'Ramón?'

His hand paused on the brake. 'Yes?'

'I want to apologise for . . . for the sun-dress I wore yesterday. It was totally unsuitable for a visit to the Marquesa. I'm sorry.'

'We did not go to see the Marquesa yesterday.'

'I know we didn't, but that doesn't alter the fact that I thought we were going there. And . . . and then you had to be extra nice and buy me that wonderful present that cost the earth. I feel awful about it, I really do.'

He said, tossing her a startled look, 'You do not like the present?'

Her voice was not quite steady. 'Of course I do. I've never had such a beautiful present, or one that could have given me more pleasure.'

'Then we have exchanged pleasure for pleasure. Your portrait of Abuela will give her much pleasure and give me pleasure also. So we will say no more about it and no more apologies. *Bien?*'

He started the car and thrust it forward in silence. Joanna retreated into her corner. She could guess what he was thinking. Why make an issue of it? His little friend was becoming a bore. He probably regarded her as a silly adolescent. What did it matter to him when he had more important matters on his mind? The air inside the car was stifling hot and the light was failing rapidly. Through the car window the dark clouds seemed to be bearing down on them aggressively.

The deluge came when they were half way to their destination, accompanied by vicious zig-zag streaks of lightning and clashes of thunder getting gradually closer. Ramón put on speed. He had switched on the headlights and the windscreen wiper was working overtime clearing away the water cascading down the windscreen. For a while there was only the sound of the car swishing through the water as it bounced off the road.

'Not afraid, are you?' Ramón tossed her a glance of concern softened by a reassuring smile. 'A freak storm, most unusual. It will soon pass.'

Joanna shook her head. How could she be afraid with him beside her? It came with cataclysmic suddenness, a violent flash of lightning that rocked the car. She covered her ears as she tensed for the inevitable clap of thunder to follow. It came at last with a frightening, chattering clap that seemed to rip the roof from the car. Thoroughly unnerved, she cringed on a muffled shriek and began to tremble. The next moment she felt the car swerve to the side of the road. The engine and lights were switched off and she was gathered gently into strong arms. She continued to tremble with the feeling that they had been spared from something terrible. Her face was pressed against Ramón, and he was whispering words of comfort to which she could not reply had her life depended upon it.

Her heart was thudding into him, and it sounded as deafening as the thunder to her startled ears. Also his nearness was making her lightheaded. He was like a magnet and she was just a poor little steel ingot forced to cling until he was ready to let her go. His arms were very tight around her and gradually her shaking ceased. As he had said, it was a freak storm, going as quickly as it had come. The lightning was becoming less violent now and the thunder fainter as it rolled away.

'It is growing lighter,' Ramón observed, slackening his hold of her a little. 'You all right now, *niña*?'

His lips brushed her hair, and she glanced up swiftly to meet that intent gaze which never failed to hold her, more powerful than words. The last few minutes held close in his arms against his strong hard body had been like a dream; a dream she wanted to cling to. It must have been her giddy reaction to his nearness that made her think he had kissed her hair, and that his voice sounded thick and a little strained.

Slowly she drew herself from his arms and looked up at the roof of the car, still intact. 'I thought we'd had it,' she said shakily.

They had stopped by banana plantations and the road was awash with water.

'Sorry this had to happen,' Ramón said as if it was his fault. 'Do you want to sit awhile, or shall we go on? The rain is easing off. Soon the sun will be out.'

'Hadn't we better go on?' she suggested, finding his presence becoming more unbearable every second. 'The Marquesa will be wondering about us.'

Ramón was not listening. He was leaning forward to take a flask of brandy from a first aid box in the glove compartment along with a small glass.

'Not for me, thanks,' Joanna exclaimed swiftly as she saw him pouring the brandy.

'It will help your nerves,' he answered, placing the glass into her hand.

Her own perception sharpened by love, Joanna knew that his personal magnetism was affecting her far more than the storm had done. The storm in her heart caused by his nearness was far more shattering as it told her that she was still hopelessly in love with a man who could not care less regarding her charms as a woman. The feeling inside her, the hopeless yearning, was so great that it was incomprehensible that he did not sense it to a certain degree. His closed expression told her nothing except to confirm that any romantic feelings he had for her were nil.

Joanna drained the glass, wishing fervently that the brandy was lethal enough to put her to sleep forever. She felt ill, and desperately near to tears. The storm, and then the final summing up of his feelings towards her, was proving too much even for her kind of courage.

'I'm much better now, but I'm longing to leave the car and breathe in the rain-washed air.'

She managed a smile of sorts as he took the glass from her, and wrapped a tissue around it for it to be washed later.

'The rain has stopped.' After a keen glance at her pale face, Ramón gazed out to the sky, clearing now of cloud like the distant mountains. 'I suppose you know that there will be much more rain in London than we see here.' He started the car and drove along the flooded road with a decorous speed. 'While your education has been a mixture of Spanish and English with the latter predominating, I must confess that I do not favour this idea of you going to London on your own,' he went on. 'I am of the opinion that Nick should go with you.'

'I think he will. If not, he's sure to go later to be there when his play opens. In any case I shall be with Laurence and Candida. Candida has offered to let me share her flat.'

'And how long do you think Candida will be there in her flat?'

A hand closed over Joanna's heart, squeezing it ruthlessly. 'I ... I have no idea. Long enough for me to stay while the play progresses, I suppose. And then Daddy will be going. Not that he'll stay long. He likes it here too much to ever want to leave it for long.'

'And you?' Ramón said slowly. 'Do you love the island too much to want to leave it for an indefinite period?'

Joanna clenched her hands and lied through pale lips, 'I don't know. I love the island very much. In fact,' she tried to laugh, and it sounded false to her ears, 'Rosita said only this morning that I was more Spanish than English. She was referring to my dress, of course.'

He did not speak for a brief space of time, and Joanna felt a desperate longing to know what lay behind his questions and his closed profile. At last, he said, 'Rosita is a remarkable woman. She is very attached to you. She will be very upset when you leave. There will be others also.'

But not you, Joanna thought, not you. 'I know,' she answered. 'But she will look after Daddy. Even if I decide to stay in London, I can come and go. After all, I shall want to see Daddy as often as I can.' When he turned briefly to raise an eyebrow in her direction, she tacked on hurriedly, 'And all my friends here, of course. I ... I suppose ... when you marry you will move to the Villa Faustino?'

'Possibly.'

'Daddy will miss you.'

Again it was so long before he replied that Joanna was beginning to wonder if he had heard her. Then he said quietly, 'And you?'

She swallowed and gazed down at the clasped hands in her lap. 'I shall miss you too.'

Sunlight flooded the car in that moment, lighting up the brilliance of the fresh, rain-washed air. Their journey was nearing its end. Ramón had not admitted that he would miss her. Did his fondness for her, his tender teasing go no further than being just neighbourly? Or was she going above her station in thinking that the Marqués Ramón de Orleron y Faustino would look upon her with favour as his future wife? As she would never know, the sensible thing to do was to do the impossible—to behave as though she had never fallen in love with him.

But Joanna had indeed set herself an impossible task. As the car drew up in the grounds of the Villa Faustino, the drive and steps leading to the entrance were still awash with running water, a fact which Ramón noticed as he left his side of the car to open Joanna's door. Without preliminaries he opened her door, thrust one arm under her knees and the other around her, and carried her effortlessly into the cool interior of the villa.

They were laughing, their heads close together, and Joanna had to quench a desire to press her smooth cheek against his tanned one as he set her down gently in the hall. Then the magic was over, leaving her body feeling strangely cold where his arms had been.

'We must not let you arrive with wet feet.' Ramón was smiling, that charming smile that melted the heart.

With the laughter brimming in her eyes, Joanna said a breathless, 'Thanks.'

As they walked together across the marble floor of the hall, she felt the eyes of Ramón's ancestors staring down their long aristocratic noses at them from the walls lining the staircase. The staircase of the Villa Faustino was very wide, beautifully carved, and swept upwards with an elegant curve. Joanna could imagine people of a bygone age gliding down the centre and scorning the help of the balustrade. Their excellent deportment so characteristic of the Spanish ladies, impeccable, courteous, graceful and serene, had no hint of the ungainly hunching of neck and shoulders. They had walked much the same as Joanna was walking now, like Ramón. Joanna had the natural deportment of a dancer, slight, erect and supple, dancing her way through a carefree and happy childhood.

Not many weeks after coming to the island, at the age of five, she had been dancing home from school when she had met Ramón. He had been watching her amusedly, or so she thought, when she had slipped and caught her ankle against a rock. But his face had been grave enough when he had knelt down beside her to take off her sandal and look at the damage. Then he had torn his handkerchief into strips, bandaged the injured part very skilfully and carried her home. That evening and many evenings afterwards, Joanna had knelt by her window staring across at Las Jacarandas, his home, wondering if she would ever see him again. She had often thought about him in the weeks that followed, not sure whether he had actually happened or that he had been part of her fantasy world. She had been full of fancies, some of them quite as real to her as her father and Rosita. The most exciting time had come later when Ramón had been home on vacation from university and had called upon her father, having seen and greatly enjoyed a play of his. Their friendship had grown from that day.

The Marquesa was in her room waiting for them, full of sparkle and ready for gossip with Joanna. After greeting her, Ramón left them together to enjoy mid-morning chocolate, and they began to talk. The Marquesa expressed her regrets that Joanna would be coming no more when the portrait was finished and requested that she should continue to visit her on occasions. She had enjoyed her visits so much and would miss them sadly.

Gently Joanna told her of her intending visit to London, but promised to call on her return. The promise was given with a heavy heart, for she knew that Ramón and Candida would probably be married by then, and the agony of seeing them together was not to be thought of. There was no swim in the pool that morning. The portrait was finished, admired, and Ramón carried Joanna's painting gear out to his car. Just before they left, the Marquesa presented her with an exquisite cameo brooch. It was old and valuable and was the Marquesa's, given to her on her twenty-first birthday by her parents. When Joanna protested against receiving so valuable a present, but the Marquesa pinned it on her dress.

'It will give me great pleasure if you will do me the honour of accepting it,' she said, kissing Joanna's flushed cheek. 'Always remember that love is giving and forgiving, *niña*, and you will be happy.'

Ramón, leaning negligently against the doorway where he had paused to watch the small ceremony after returning from taking her belongings to his car, smiled mockingly at Joanna's flushed cheeks.

'We have forgotten one thing,' he said, lunging forward to stroll towards them. 'I have not paid Joanna for the portrait. We had, I believe, an agreement?' His eyebrows lifted tantalising and he reached for her hand to place something into it. 'One escudo, the price you demanded for painting the portrait.' He closed Joanna's fingers over the coin and turned to address his grandmother with a mocking inflection. His hand still held Joanna's as it closed over her own. 'Joanna insisted upon no payment for your portrait and we finally came to an agreement. Is that not so, Juana *mia*?'

For a moment Joanna was at a loss. She had almost forgotten the escudo they had settled upon. The warm grasp of his hand was reawakening the sense of vanished delight his touch gave to her. The old endearment coming from his lips was more than unsettling too, and she felt the swift colour rising up afresh in her face. All her reserves were mustered to recover her composure beneath Ramón's mocking regard.

'Thank you, Ramón,' she said with dignity. Her hand was trembling under his as she drew it away.

The return journey to the Villa Rosario was accomplished in the shortest time as Ramón had a business appointment at midday. Joanna saw him go with the feeling that he was already on his way out of her life. In a way she was relieved that the morning had ended so quickly. She had already been torn apart by too many emotions and could not wait to reach the sanctuary of her own room. The escudo was still clutched in her hand as she regained the shelter of her room unheard. During the return journey she had sat for the most part silent, subjecting her feelings to a rigorous control. Now freed of Ramón's tantalising presence, she drew a deep, slow breath as if tension inside her slowly relaxed. Unclenching her hand, she looked down for a long time at the escudo in her palm, then bending her head she kissed it.

She changed into the blue denim for lunch, which proved to be a kind of celebration. Nick had finished his play and the rehearsals were, at last, performed to his satisfaction.

There was to be a party that evening, the last before Candida and Laurence left for London. An invitation was sent to Ramón, and Candida wore an excited air as though she had been waiting for this to happen. That afternoon Joanna drove Candida and Laurence to Las Palmas to do some last-minute shopping. She bought things for the party and left the other two to do what shopping they wanted. They all met for tea at a little café, where Laurence presented her with a bracelet of lucky charms and Candida gave her a powder compact. They had bought boxes of cigars for Nick.

Ramón did not come to the party that night. He was away in Tenerife on business. Nick had invited some of his friends and the party was a success. It was late when the festivities came to an end, and Joanna was the first to go upstairs to her room after the last guest left. Her brightness during the evening had been of the brittle kind, with her senses forever on the alert for the sound of Ramón's car. Even now, late though it was, she could hardly believe that he was not coming. Right until going to her room she had been waiting for him to arrive. He would walk in on a sweep of mountain air, his skin glowing and tanned by the Spanish sun, his brilliant smile giving his skin a flattering darker hue. And she would try in vain to control the foolish beating of her heart as he strode towards her with a feline grace. But he had not come.

Joanna had given him up when suddenly, unaccountably, she heard the sound of his car, then voices. Seated at the dressing table, she put her hairbrush down with shaking fingers. A struggle was taking place inside her. Her face stared back at her from the mirror, all eyes. If only she had the courage to go downstairs to tell him how she felt about him! But it would take more than courage. It would be utterly reckless for there was no doubt at all how he would react. He would weather it as calmly and undramatically as he had weathered her appearance half clad for her visit to the Marquesa that morning. Even though her heart rebelled against leaving him with Candida, Joanna knew that she could not face him that night. Her hurt was too great. Her memory winged back to the many good times she had shared with Ramón, knowing that no one could take them away from her, not even Candida. So she stifled the wild longing to seek him out.

The sudden tap on her door swung her round with startled eyes to see her father enter. 'Ah, so you haven't gone to bed yet. I want to talk to you.'

He seated himself opposite Joanna near to the bed and watched her unblinkingly. His calm matter-of-fact entrance had calmed her down considerably and she was able to speak naturally.

'Did I hear Ramón's car?' she asked.

'You did.' Nick crossed his legs and lay back in his chair. 'He's come to say goodbye for a while. He's just come back from a business conference at Tenerife and he's off in a few hours to attend another. He's saying his goodbyes to Candida and Laurence, as he won't see them again before they go back.'

Joanna picked up a jar of cold cream and applied a little to her face surprised to find her hand quite steady. 'Did . . . did he say anything about going to see your play in London?' The pause required a considerable time for her to make the effort to continue. 'He's . . . he's sure to want to see Candida in the play.'

Nick shrugged. 'I suppose he's making all the arrangements with her now before he leaves. Laurence and I left them together. But that isn't what I've come to talk to you about. I've been thinking—you won't have much of a time going to share Candida's flat in London while she and Laurence are both at rehearsals for the play. Added to that I don't like the thought of you going around London alone. So I've decided to go with you. What do you say to us booking in at a hotel and seeing the sights again together? I shan't be needed every day at the theatre, and I haven't forgotten how to dance. Between us we could paint the town. What do you say?'

For long moments Joanna stared at her father, wondering if he had guessed about her love for Ramón. Was he offering her the alternative of staying with Candida where she would have to witness the lovers meeting when Ramón called, or did he want her with him? Either way it was a reprieve. It had not occurred to her until now what she would have been letting herself in for by sharing a flat with Candida.

Suddenly she was across the room and flinging herself into his arms.

'Oh, Daddy!' she cried, torn between laughter and tears. 'I'd love to go to a hotel with you. It'll be wonderful.'

'Hey now, don't strangle me!' he protested as she landed upon his knee to fling her arms around his neck. Then he laughed. 'That's settled, then.'

CHAPTER ELEVEN

As it happened Joanna did not travel to London with Candida and Laurence. Nick had things to do before he left and it was a fortnight later when they went. In the meantime there had been no sign of word from Ramón. He was not at home. Joanna gazed across at Las Jacarandas for the last time with a tenderness and regret overlain by a craving for release. By going away she would gradually clear her mind and heart of Ramón. It would be like tearing herself out by the roots, but she had to know where she was going. She had to escape from seeing him, from hearing his voice, and from wanting him.

Her future stretched before her, not widening into blissful horizons with Ramón but narrowing, dwindling and shrinking into the final acceptance of life without him. He could return home any time and she had to make a getaway before then. If she did not go now she would never go. Everything, her love for the island, the primitive beauty, the peace of the Villa Rosario, the loving care lavished upon her by Rosita, and last but not least Ramón, would hold her until her last breath. She had to built a new life for herself. Without thinking too far ahead it might be possible for her to make a success of her portrait painting in London. She might even go on to Paris.

The bouquet of flowers tied with ribbon, twelve exquisite roses, was given to her on her arrival at their hotel in London. From Ramón.

'But how did he know we were here?' she asked Nick in some confusion.

'I gave him the name of this hotel and the time we would arrive when he came to the Villa Rosario to say goodbye to Candida and Laurence. I suppose he ordered a similar bouquet for Candida when she arrived back in London.'

His last words swept across her pleasure of the flowers

like a biting east wind. For Nick's benefit, she smiled. 'Isn't that just like Ramón?' she said flippantly, and walked with her father to the lift waiting to take them to their rooms.

London was no less enchanting or exciting than Joanna had vaguely remembered it. She knew that romantic ideas tend to fade on contact with the reality, but her bright eyes, between long lashes, dwelt with pleasure on the London crowds, the traffic jams, the historical buildings, and the beautiful parks. Men, on passing, returned her entranced look with one of great interest. Her legs, long, slim, tanned, her pretty ankles as delicately formed as her deliciously curved body, her piquant face, animated and enchanting, arrested more than one pair of masculine feet in their long stride.

Las Palmas was as remote as if she had been away for an age. Only the memory of Ramón was painful. Rehearsals for the play were going well, with Nick having put in most of the groundwork by putting the two leads through their paces beforehand. Laurence and Candida were occupied most of the day with rehearsals at the theatre and part of the evenings too. The four of them went out to a show or a meal occasionally, but most of the time Joanna spent with her father. Like his daughter, Nick was restless and haunted by memories—memories, Joanna knew, of her mother. So, as he had suggested, they lived it up, dancing most nights until the small hours.

Then as the opening night of the play drew nearer, Nick was inclined to haunt the theatre. The producer, a man familiar with Nick Main plays, was more than enthusiastic about his latest one. 'The best you've done, Nick,' he said. 'That's saying something, considering how successful your other plays have been to date.' As an afterthought, he added, 'Can't think why you haven't come to an opening night before. That island must have something special.'

It has, thought Joanna—Ramón. She wondered where he was and what he was doing. He had not been to see Candida, who was in no way downhearted, which could mean that they had some kind of understanding between them. Mindful of not causing Nick any kind of misgivings concerning the success of his play, Ramón had probably put off their engagement until after the opening night.

When it came, Joanna shared her father's excitement and slight apprehension. They both knew that public opinion had changed during the last two years, and the fact that Nick's last play was still running successfully in London was no guarantee that the new one would be a winner. The previous night, Joanna had slept well and had awakened feeling completely refreshed. Her room was quiet after the early clinking of milk bottles and the sound of cars setting off for some known destination. The morning was sunny, too enticing to stay in bed, and there was a cheeky sparrow on her windowsill chirping for crumbs. She rang for room service and requested breakfast. It came promptly, along with a letter. The young man, who had not ceased to gaze upon her with blatant admiration from the moment she had arrived at the hotel, told her that he had been passing the reception desk when the mail was being sorted and had brought her letter up with him.

Joanna smiled, glanced at the envelope and recognised Rosita's handwriting. 'Thanks,' she said, and was annoyed with herself for blushing.

When he had gone, she pattered to the window with a piece of soft bread roll for the sparrow who was waiting with tiny, bright, expectant and hopeful eyes. Then she opened the letter.

Rosita began by saying that she hoped Joanna was wearing wool next to her skin as she believed that a woollen vest was essential in the English climate, also that she was eating all the right things. Then, after reporting the local news, she went on to say that the Señor Marqués was back at Las Jacarandas and something appeared to be in the wind. There were rumours that he was going to be married at last. He had spent a great deal of time taking the golden-haired Englishwoman around the island and it was rumoured that he was going to London to see her in Nick's play at the opening night. She hoped that Joanna was enjoying herself and everyone, including herself, missed her very much. Joanna felt something cold squeeze her heart.

Had Rosita guessed that she loved Ramón? Her quick dark eyes never missed a thing where her Joanna was concerned. She stared down at the letter, sensing soft waves of compassion rippling towards her from between the written lines.

Raising her eyes, slightly misty, she gazed out at the thick green foliage of the plane tree outside her window, catching facets of light from the morning sun. Was it a symbol of her life in the future? Were the thick, dark shadows among the glossy leaves a warning of dark days to come? One day soon the leaves would rust into autumn. Gradually, the branches would become stark and barren in the winter winds, like her life without Ramón. Joanna walked over to the window, her heart a dead thing in her breast that only he could bring to life. His name ran through her head like a haunting refrain. She had only to pick up the telephone near her bed to contact him, to hear his beloved voice.

It gave her quite a turn when the telephone rang at that moment, setting up all kinds of emotions inside her. It was a moment or two before she could gather up the courage to answer it.

'Hi there,' Laurence said on a bright note. 'Remember me? I never seem to have you to myself these days, what with the play and Nick always being there. Not that there's much time today, with the play opening tonight. But as we aren't going to the theatre until this afternoon to take a last run through the play, I thought you and I might go out this morning and then have lunch together. What do you say?'

Her smile was wistful had he but seen it, her tone gentle. 'I'd love to spend the morning with you, Laurence,' she answered steadily. 'Daddy will be at the theatre this morning, something to do with the scenery for the play. What time shall I see you?'

'Ten o'clock be all right? We could go on the Thames and have lunch there? Anything you say.'

'I'd love that. I'll be ready.'

The framed patch of sky in her window was already a milky blue, promising heat. Deliberating on what to wear, her eyes alighted upon the delicate lilac gingham foursome of over-shirt, minute shorts, bikini and bra which she had worn on the morning that Ramón had bought her the stereo and records. Why not? Simply had to wipe out his image. This time she would wear it for Laurence.

'You look absolutely stunning,' was his comment when she met him in the foyer of the hotel. 'A delight to the eye.'

He linked his arm in hers and they walked out into the bright sunlight. The way he had of combining friendship with a touch of humility endeared her to him. It was in direct contrast to Ramón's more masterful ways. While Laurence would never make the blood thunder through her body or his touch fill her with an aching longing to belong, at least he made life pleasant and bearable. As her life quietened down into some kind of routine, strange things could happen, like growing more fond of Laurence, and forgetting Ramón in the process.

It was pleasant on the Thames, with the slow flow of the water lapping gently against the side of the boat, the passing pleasure craft decorated with reclining brown bodies on their decks, the sun caressing their limbs.

Joanna's hair was a shining, windblown mass around her neat head, her face an echanting curve from brow to chin meandering down to the sunny hollows at the base of her slim throat. Beneath the lilac shirt, her small breasts were high and round, her long legs a smooth honey tan, as she grew somnolent and nostalgic in the sun. She was oblivious of the admiring glances directed at her, from Laurence, from anyone.

'You're the kind of girl men spend their life wishing would walk past their office, their flat door, their restaurant table, their gate or their seat in the park. And here you are dazzling me with your charms,' Laurence whispered in her ear. He had taken off his jacket and was sprawling beside her studying her lazily, his eyes narrowing on the slenderness of her waist, the enchanting curves of her hips and shoulders as he felt an overpowering desire to crush her in his arms. 'I love you.'

Those last three words pierced her absorption in something far away. She turned to look sadly at him. Her eyes were shadowy between the long, dark lashes, her face wistful, her mouth mobile and tentatively expressive.

'Thank you,' she answered as if he had just handed her a sandwich. 'I'm very fond of you, Laurence, but I don't love you in the way that I think you mean.'

'You could do one day,' he insisted, knowing that his brief ecstasy was over and that she loved someone else. Why else would she be so wistful about it? He looked at her with a shrewd and interested eye. 'Who's the lucky man?' he asked, lifting a brow.

But Joanna would not be drawn. 'I'm a dreamer,' she said, 'in love with an image, like those men you've just mentioned.' Which was quite true, she argued to herself. Only Ramón had walked right past with his eyes on someone else—Candida.

So she strung Laurence along for the rest of that morning on affectionate platitudes, knowing that she was fast becoming a master at dissembling Laurence's confession of his love had recharged her ego, but she still pined for Ramón. Over lunch they had talked about the play and the fact that the theatre was booked up to capacity. Then they had gone on to talk of other things, how long she was staying in London and if she would accompany him on a visit to his parents' one weekend. She would like the farm, he was sure.

When at last Laurence became, quite abruptly, aware that he would have to leave for the theatre directly the boat docked, Joanna felt that she did not want him to go. But she kissed his cheek and reminded him not to work too hard that afternoon because of what was to follow.

It was then that he delivered the bombshell, quite casually, with no possible knowledge of the explosion which followed. They had already parted when he suddenly swung round to say on an afterthought, 'I forgot to tell you—I bumped into Candida on my way to your hotel this morning. She said Ramón is here in London. Apparently he's come to see the first night of the play.'

Joanna was thankful that Laurence continued on his way

directly after telling her, for she was sure her expression would have given her away. As it was he missed the sudden paleness of her cheeks, the bleakness of her eyes as she cringed as from a mortal blow. Ramón was in London and he had not let her know! He had preferred Candida to meet him. She, who had known him for most of her life, had been cast aside for someone he had only known for a matter of weeks. He was so much in love that nothing or no one else counted. But was not that how she, Joanna, loved him, to the exclusion of all else? Lucky Candida!

For the rest of the day right up to when she had to change to go to the theatre with Nick for the opening of his play, Joanna was numb. But she knew it was only deadened nerves crushed with shock which, when they began to feel again, would hurt unbearably. They were to occupy a box at the side of the stage, and Nick had insisted upon buying her an expensive model dress for the occasion. After a visit to the hairdresser and manicurist, Joanna put on the dress mechanically. It was a delicious dream in pure silk chiffon. Palest eau-de-nil and écru with a flower design, it had a heart-shaped neckline and wide sleeves. The sash hugging her slender waist was a mesh of mother-of-pearl to match the broad necklet around her slender neck, and the bracelet on her wrist. Her make-up was fragile, a hint of colour on her eyelids and a peach lipstick. Her hair had been allowed to fall naturally in silky abundance around her face.

Coming to her room to see if she was ready, her father had stood to stare in astonishment in the doorway. His face paled for a moment.

Hoarsely, he said, 'You look so much like your mother that you take my breath away. Like her, you have that air of glamour about you without knowing it. It's all there with an air of calm and serenity that was instantly appealing.' He sighed nostalgically. 'You're very beauti . . .' Nick pulled himself up short and smiled proudly at his daughter. 'But there, I mustn't flatter you too much. I'm sure you'll have a surfeit of that this evening at the theatre. Ready?'

Joanna nodded and came forward to slip a hand through

his arm. 'You're looking more than handsome yourself, and kind of distinguished in evening dress with that darling little beard. I suppose you have butterflies in your tum. I know I have!' Her look was tender.

He smiled down at her and patted her hand. 'First night nerves,' he admitted. 'I only hope Candida and Laurence aren't suffering from them too much.'

Candida's name brought back a rush of feeling. They were in the taxi on their way to the theatre when Joanna found the courage to mention Ramón.

'Did you know Ramón was in London?' she asked, smoothing the folds of her skirt with trembling fingers.

'Yes, he's coming to the theatre later,' he replied, and Joanna was silent.

It was clear from the first act that the play would be an enormous success. It was filled with brilliant repartee and wit, the action swift and altogether enjoyable. It began as a sophisticated comedy and gradually worked its way through to drama existing in the present day. The refreshing change from the violence and sex which had been thrust upon audiences in recent years was received with a standing ovation at the end.

Candida and Laurence were superb. Like the rest of the cast they seemed to be inspired and held the audience spellbound. Joanna surfaced from the first act to scan the audience from her box in search of Ramón, but he was not there. Then her father began to talk about the play.

'Seems to be going down well,' he said, looking round at the packed theatre. 'I haven't seen Ramón. Have you?' She shook her head and he went on with a frown, 'It isn't like him to be so late. He was to join us here in our box and go with us after the show for a celebration dinner.'

Joanna was silent, wondering why he had not told her before about Ramón joining them. Already her stomach had begun to churn at the thought of seeing him again. The lights had been lowered and the curtain was rising on the second act when someone entered their box behind her. The sudden melting of her bones told her that it was Ramón, and she was thankful for the respite provided by the play before she had to greet him.

When the lights went up again at the end of the second act, Joanna was composed enough to turn around in her seat to greet him. And there he was his lips curving over white teeth in that familiar shattering smile. Her eyes, sharpened by love, looked for some change in him. He still radiated that dynamic vitality like a kind of miraculous manifestation resulting from the heat of the Spanish sun. He had not altered. At the same time she sensed something different about him, for he was looking at her with as shrewd and interested an eye that she had ever seen. Their eyes seemed to collide and lock, and Joanna was unable to tear hers away.

Nick said, 'Ramón arrived too late to join us for the first act, and stayed at the back of the auditorium with a friend until the interval.'

'Needless to say,' said Ramón, 'I enjoyed it very much. So did Miguel, from the Spanish Embassy, an old friend of mine from university days. Like myself, he did not allow for the amount of traffic on the road. I must apologise for being late. And how are you both?'

Futilely, Joanna wished she could allow her face to reflect the poignant entreaty of her thoughts, to look into his eyes with her own misty with the beauty of her love. But with the subdued lighting creating a soft halo around her head, her eyes luminous, she reacted in the way he would expect her to act when greeting an old friend, her smile as delighted as his own. Again she met his eyes, found them unreadable, and said lightly, 'We're living it up, Daddy and I. We have a lot to make up for.'

Nick grimaced. 'You have, you mean. The only thing I shall have to make up for is sleep when I return home!' He smiled fondly at Ramón, wide-shouldered, dark and keen-eyed in his immaculate evening suit. 'Funny thing, when I was in Las Palmas I looked on London as my home. Now I'm here I look on Las Palmas as my home. I can't wait to go back.'

Ramón smiled delightedly. 'That is as it should be,' he

agreed. 'I would be most upset to lose one of my best friends.' He raised a black silky brow. 'So the success of your play will not persuade you to stay in London. You will be returning to Las Palmas soon?'

'As soon as possible.'

'And Juana *mia*? Will she be going back with you?' Ramón looked at Joanna as he spoke. His dark eyes were mocking the sudden heat in her cheeks.

Joanna trembled inwardly with the violence of emotion his endearment had evoked. He had spoken with the assurance of a man who knew where his own happiness lay. Life presented few problems for the Marqués de Orleron y Faustino. He knew what he wanted from life and set out to procure it.

It was Nick who answered. 'I think not. At least, not for a time. Is that not so, Joanna?' he queried, eyeing her flushed face thoughtfully.

'That's right,' she replied, surprised to find herself speaking so coolly when all her pulses were hammering. 'There's no reason why I shouldn't take a flat of my own and ... and paint again.'

Ramón's dark eyes travelled slowly, lazily over the perfection of her golden brown skin, pale and creamy in the subdued lighting. Soft-voiced, gentle and sweet with an untouched air about her, Joanna was blissfully unaware of her own feminine charms—so much so that she misinterpreted Ramón's cynical regard.

'I would say,' he drawled with a hint of satire, 'and I am sure Nick will agree with me, that you look enchanting enough to sit for a portrait yourself instead of being the artist.' His eyes narrowed, hardened. 'The London scene suits you. I have never seen you look more poignantly lovely. However, I would like to utter a word of warning. London is not Las Palmas. It is well that you have the protection of Laurence.'

'I can take care of myself,' Joanna answered, hating him in the moment for treating her like a child. Nick was looking from one to the other in mild amusement.

'I'm afraid, my dear,' he said, 'Ramón is inclined to regard you as being more Spanish than English and is therefore in favour of a duenna. Is that not so, Ramón?'

Ramón's eyes glittered. 'And why not? Any great metropolis is a jungle of snares set for the unwary. Your daughter, Nick, is an innocent abroad. I would say she definitely needs protection.'

For what seemed an age to Joanna, he held her gaze. Then he turned to talk to Nick of other matters as if she no longer existed.

Minutes later, the curtain went up on the third and last act. Most of the audience had kept their seats during the last interval in a buzz of conversation as they discussed the play. Nick Main's magic, his subtle understanding of human nature, his mastery in putting it over to an audience in brilliant dialogue and exciting climax, had left the audience hungering for more.

Joanna forgot for the moment her inner tumult, and lost herself once more in the magic of the play. The end was an exciting and satisfactory one, giving her no time to think of problems. The final curtain was the signal for a standing ovation from an excited audience. Their voices demanding the author, held a dreamlike quality for Joanna, who left her seat before the spotlight could be centred on their box. Hurrying back in the shadows in order to leave her father to take his bow, she stumbled into Ramón's arms.

For esctatic moments she was held against him as Nick delivered his brief speech in which he thanked all concerned for working so hard to make his play a success. And because that ecstasy was underlaid by the unbearable pain of unrequited love, she had to push herself free from his arms. There was no time to see his reaction, for he was joining in the applause as the members of the cast lined the stage to take a final bow with Nick looking down at them.

Joanna felt near to screaming. Elated though she was at the success of the play, mad as she was about Ramón, she would have given anything to get away from everything. It was impossible for her to meet Ramón after tonight, for this was the moment he had been waiting for, the moment when the success of the play was assured. From now on Candida had only to stay in the lead until a substitute could be found to take her place, then she and Ramón would be married. Joanna knew that there was to be a celebration party for all the cast. Nick had planned on giving it even if the play had not been a success. It would be impossible for her to go. What courage she could muster to carry her through the rest of the evening would crack under the strain of seeing Ramón with Candida, perhaps hearing him make the announcement of their engagement.

When once she had established herself in London to begin painting in earnest it was quite possible that her memories of Ramón would deteriorate until his whole image, his lazy relaxed charm, his virile magnetic personality; his disturbing good looks, his endearing but arrogant demands, would become blurred with the mists of time. He had been a part of her growing up. He belonged to her childhood dreams. He had taught her many things, and all of them good. It had not been his fault that she had fallen in love with him. So many other women had; she was only one of many. Yet all the others had been luckier than Joanna Main, for they had known what it was to have him as a lover. For a brief spell they had become part of him. She never had.

Joanna became aware of the audience leaving their seats. Her father turned to face Ramón and herself. A smile had replaced the look of strain on his face. Only now did Joanna realise how deeply he had felt her mother's death. The next moment her arms were around his neck. Tears blurred her eyes as she kissed his cheek. If only her mother could have been there.

'Oh, Daddy,' she cried, 'I'm so proud of you! It was wonderful!'

Nick felt the soft fragrance of her hair against his face as she buried her face in his neck, and the dampness of her happy tears. Slowly he put his hands upon her shoulders and putting her a little distance away from him, looked down into her tear-drenched face.

'Hey now, no tears,' he demanded with a fond grimace. 'We're going to celebrate, not weep. Come on, dry those tears.' He gave her his handkerchief, and placed an arm around her as she dried her face. It was comforting to have a shoulder to cry on, she thought. The only heartbreaking thing about it was that the closeness between Nick and herself had come when they were on the brink of parting, perhaps for years. It seemed to Joanna in that moment that all the past was weighing down upon her head until the pain became unbearable.

Nick took the handkerchief she offered. His face tightened with anxiety. 'Are you all right? You look as pale as a sheet. Sit down.'

Joanna shook her head vehemently. 'No, no, I'm all right, Daddy. Don't fuss. It's . . . just a bad head.'

Nick frowned, unconvinced. 'I've never known you have a headache before. I don't feel too chipper myself.' He looked at Ramón standing silent in the shadows, and smiled apologetically. 'It's all those late nights. We don't have your excellent physique.'

'And I do not possess your talent for giving people so much pleasure through your plays,' Ramón answered. 'Congratulations on a well deserved success. I thoroughly enjoyed it.'

Nick was pleased. 'Thanks. What did you think of Candida? Quite a girl, wasn't she? The part might have been created for her—Laurence too. I have a feeling that you had a hand in the presenting of the two wonderful baskets of flowers to them.' He turned his head to look at Joanna as she touched his arm.

Perfectly composed now but looking a little strained, she whispered,

'Would you mind, Daddy, if I didn't go on with you to the party? I have a terrible head, and it will be a relief to lie down quietly in my room.'

Nick patted her hand as it lay on her arm. 'Of course, if that's how you feel. Sure you wouldn't like me to ring up the doctor for some pain-killing tablets? They might help to give you a good night's rest.'

'No, Daddy, please. I'll be all right.'

'I'll see you to your hotel.' It was Ramón who spoke, and Joanna's heart gave a sickening jolt.

'No, no. I insist that you join the others along with Daddy for the party. I can get a taxi to the hotel.' Joanna gave a piteous look at her father. 'Sorry, Daddy. Have a nice time. I'll be feeling fine in the morning.'

The next moment she was running from the box to join the last of the guests going down the stairs. Outside the theatre taxis were drawing up in response to requests from the theatregoers, and Joanna looked about her in desperation as one taxi after another was commandeered under her nose.

Instinct had told her of Ramón's presence behind her even as the taxi slid to a halt in front of her. There was that familiar breathless feeling in her chest and the reaction of thundering heartbeats. Only the grasp of his fingers on her arm could create such havoc to her nervous system as he opened the door of the taxi and helped her in. Giving the taxi driver the name of her hotel, he slipped in beside her.

'You didn't have to come with me, Ramón,' she said in a small voice, drawing into her corner. She felt beaten and terribly conscious of spoiling his evening and her father's too. Words rushed out. 'I feel awful, spoiling your evening.'

'My evening is not spoiled . . . yet,' he answered, and she understood the pause before his last word. He would be going back again to the party. Why on earth had he come unless he felt he owed it to Nick to allow him to go to his party knowing that Joanna was being taken care of? She could not explain his behaviour in any other way. Candida would not like it. Neither did she! Her head was throbbing and one glance at his profile showed he was deep in thought. Even when she was with him she could not hold his attention, for he seemed to be miles away in his thoughts. What an idiot she had been to ever think that he would look upon her as his *marquesa*! Not when he could, at the crook of a lean finger, have his pick of dozens of beautiful women, some of them titled, most of them wealthy.

In five minutes they had reached the hotel in silence. Ramón helped her out and walked with her into the foyer.

At the reception desk he waited while she collected her key and went with her into the lift. Her room was on the second floor, and Joanna had hardly expected Ramón to come all the way with her to her door. As he had piloted her into the lift, her upward gaze at his dark face was rather startled, but he seemed unaware of it. There were several more people in the lift and she had to stand quite close to him. When the lift jerked to a stop on the first floor his hands fastened on her upper arms as she was flung back against him. And there he held her until they reached the second floor.

Supported by the firmness of his touch and his air of impregnability, Joanna was ready to scream. She was sure that if it had not been for a couple still left in the lift to continue the journey upwards, she would have done. Some things are impossible to bear, and Ramón's touch was becoming one of them—so much so that when his hands released her as the lift reached her floor, she stepped out of it quickly and made for her door. When she reached it her hands were trembling so much that she doubted if she could fit the key in the lock.

'Goodnight, Ramón. Thanks for seeing me to my door,' she said pointedly, without turning round knowing that he was right behind her.

There was no reply and she swung to face him, key in hand. She looked pale and a pulse beat in the delicate skin at her temple, but her manner was controlled, even cool. He was so close he might have knocked her over as she swung round to face him. His face, like his chiselled mouth, showed no expression. The next moment he had taken her firmly around the waist to lift her to one side and taken possession of her door key. Then he was opening the door.

By now Joanna was quivering and uncertain how to handle him. He was acting very peculiarly and completely out of character as he inclined his dark head for her to precede him into the room. He had taken the key out of the door and kept it in his hand. She could hardly believe it, but he was following her into her room. Crossing to the dressing table on trembling legs, Joanna put her evening purse down and turned to face him. To her horror, he was striding across the room to the telephone beside her bed.

'What are you going to do?' she asked weakly.

'Call reception for a doctor. You need a tranquilliser. I cannot think what Nick has been thinking of to allow you to get in this exhausted condition,' he said curtly. 'You've done nothing but tremble since I arrived at the theatre, and you look exhausted.'

Joanna suddenly could not take any more. 'I am not exhausted, and will you please put down that telephone! All I have is a bad head, and you have to go ringing up doctors for tranquillisers! If you don't leave me alone, I shall scream!'

He put down the telephone and turned to eye her coolly. 'It's Laurence, is it not? You are upset because his time has been taken up more or less with the play. It is difficult for the young to accept parting when they are so much in love.' His deep voice became tender although his dark eyes held no particular expression in them. 'I was wrong to escort you home. I ought to have given Laurence the privilege.'

Joanna glared at him across her bed and turned her back. 'Go, will you! Just go and leave me alone.' She had clenched her hands and was now lifting them to her face. 'Get out!'

For the next few seconds the room held a listening quality, and Joanna felt it bristling with her rudeness. But she was past caring. All she wanted to do was to lie down and die. Ramón spoke again somewhere near to the door.

'I will send Laurence to you,' he said quietly.

To Joanna, who was aching to be alone with her grief, this came as the last straw. Twisting around to face him, her mouth compressed, her eyes bright with unshed tears, she cried, 'All right, send Laurence . . . send Daddy . . . send them all! What do I care? Now get out! I hate you . . . Do you hear? I hate you!'

With tears streaming down her face, she flung herself face down on to her bed and crumpled up into convulsive weeping. She did not hear him go until the key turned in the lock, Then there was silence. She almost went hysterical, then when it occurred to her that he had locked her in because he was convinced that she did need a doctor.

Joanna wept on unrestrainedly for several minutes. Then she stopped crying and grew quiet as the bed beside her gave way to an added weight. Lifting her face and turning her head, she drew a finger beneath each eye with a child-like gesture and stared up into Ramón's dark eyes. He was sitting beside her on the bed. It was too much—that he should see her like this with her face all swollen and blotched with weeping.

Joanna turned her head away quickly, her hair serving as a curtain to hide the tears which, idiotically, were again beyond her control. She felt him take her shoulder and turn her gently towards him. Taking her chin with one hand, he swept her hair back from her hot face with the other. Then he produced his handkerchief and wiped her face very gently.

'Now relax,' he said, drawing her head against him. 'Then we might be able to get somewhere. Just rest quietly.'

Gently his hand moved over the back of her head until the dry sobs coming from deep inside her like hiccups gradually ceased. They stayed like that for a long time. Joanna was silent, not because he had told her to be but because she was hopelessly beyond words. The more she tried to question his actions, the more confused she became. Why had he not gone after she had been so rude to him? Why had he locked her door? And Candida? What about Candida, knowing nothing of all this, and waiting for him at the celebration party? Clasped in his arms with all his warmth and vitality seeping into her, Joanna tried to cope with her giddy reaction to his nearness.

It would be so easy to betray her feelings, to see the calm way with which he would deal with an embarrassing situation. Never that. She would die first. If only time would stand still and these precious moments go on for ever! Ramón spoke first, with the fragrance of her hair against his lips.

'Better now?' he asked.

She mumbled into his chest and, unable to bear his closeness, freed herself from his arms and springing to her feet, walked to the window where she stood with her back to him.

'I'm sorry for behaving so childishly,' she said to the tree outside her window. 'I don't know what got into me, unless it was the . . . strain of Daddy's play, wondering if it would be a success . . . and other things.'

Ramón was leaning elegantly on her bed, supported by an elbow. His lean, dark face was inscrutable, his dark eyes keen and probing.

'You said just now that Nick's play and other things had brought on a sudden burst of emotion,' he said quietly. 'Shall we begin with these . . . er . . . other things? What are they? Perhaps I can help.'

'I would rather not discuss them,' Joanna answered in a small voice. 'I have to work out my own solution.'

'Does Laurence enter into it? I am asking because I might be able to help.' Joanna did not answer. She flinched knowing that the barrier of misunderstanding between them could never be lifted. She felt helpless. 'All right,' Ramón went on. 'You said about continuing with your painting. Have you settled upon somewhere suitable, some studio?'

'No. I'd rather not talk about it.'

'So. You do not want to talk about Laurence or your painting. I will be more specific. Do you love Laurence?'

Joanna stiffened. 'You've no right to ask me so personal a question!' She covered her face with he hands. 'Why must you insist upon torturing me like this? I don't ask you personal questions, I never have.'

'Ask me one now.' Suddenly he was standing behind her, his hands on her shoulders. 'Go on,' he urged, 'ask me one.'

Joanna cringed beneath the warmth of his hands sending all kinds of vibrations through her. Her hands were covering her face as she stood with her back to him. He had drawn her back against him and his last words, deep and disturbing, had been spoken above her ear, his breath warm on her cheek.

Joanna's heart dipped and almost stopped. He was gripping her shoulders in a cruel way which she found, strangely enough, oddly satisfying. She wanted him to hurt her just as she wanted him to want her passionately, if only to prove that he no longer regarded her as a child but a grown woman. But she had forgotten Candida, who was waiting at that very moment for him to join her at the celebration party.

Her voice was husky with control. 'You'd better go. Candida will be waiting for you.'

'For me?' he sounded startled. 'Why should Candida be waiting for me?'

Joanna answered with difficulty. 'That's a rather odd question, coming from the man she's to marry!'

'Marry Candida? What is this?' He swung her round to face him, dark eyes glittering, mouth compressed. 'And why should you think I am going to marry Candida, when I asked her to bring you and Laurence along each time we went out together, when I persuaded Abuela to have her portrait painted, although she hated it, to give me the excuse of spending time with you? I was most disturbed when your English visitors arrived to upset all my plans, for you and me.' He gazed down into her startled face and his hands began to caress her throat, tilting back her head. 'How could I not be upset when my Juana was not yet awakened to what love could mean? I told myself that the sudden appearance of the fair-haired Englishman could make a deep impression on her untutored mind. Not only that, my Juana with her sunny smile, her honey brown hair and maddeningly clear, beautiful eyes, a skin reminding one of a ripe apricot, and a beautiful body which I wanted her to keep for me, was already enamoured with this Laurence because he was an Englishman.' He suddenly looked so humble, so unlike himself, as he murmured, 'Why did you choose to go off with Laurence when you might have joined Candida and me?'

Joanna, who had gone pale and red in turn, was glowing like a rose as she tried to take in what he was saying. Candida had never passed on any of his invitations to her and Laurence, and only she, Joanna, knew why. And she was not going to tell him. If Candida loved him half as much as she did herself, she could only feel a deep compassion for her.

Her answer was another question, one that even now was hard to believe.

'You ... you mean ... you aren't in love with Candida?' she gasped.

The fine nostrils of his handsome nose distended. He glowered, his teeth tight. 'I have never in my life been in love, not truly in love with anyone excepting Juana *mia*.' His brown fingers caressed her warm cheek and he grew tender. 'But you were only a child. You are still, with your little pointed face, your large trusting eyes and your lovely mouth just asking to be kissed. Also there were the stars in your eyes when you spoke of England, and I had to let you go, to make up your own mind what you wanted.' His dark eyes burned deep into hers. 'Now I am telling myself that the time has come to declare my love. You are miserable because you have discovered that you are Juana *mia* after all and not an English miss as you had believed.' He picked up her hands to kiss each palm. 'Such clever hands, but so small to hold my heart and all my love.'

He was kissing her eyelids, her flushed cheeks, the warm hollow in her throat, and his arms tightened around her as they had done in her dreams.

Bemused and bewildered, Joanna was convinced that this too was a dream; that his embrace filling her with such swooning bliss would vanish at any moment, leaving her to wake up to the stark reality of life without him. For a moment she tensed and trembled as his mouth sought and found her own. Then her bones seemed to melt and her arms crept up around his neck to cling close and fiercely loving. So they stood locked together in long moments of ecstasy. Her hands moved over the back of his bent head, loving the feel of him against her, his lean hard body, bruising lips—close, passionate and loving.

He said, 'You've changed.'

Her dishevelled blush deepened. 'I haven't changed. I adore you, I always will.'

'I mean, you've grown up. You're terribly exciting—all woman.' He smiled on a flash of white teeth. 'That was what I was waiting for, because you see, Juana *mia*, I am no boy but a man who has waited a long time for the woman of his heart to love him as he loves her.'

Joanna eyed him primly. 'You've always regarded me as a child, never as a woman, and . . . and here I am with my face all tear-stained and my hair a mess, and you tell me I've grown up!'

His look was one of tender mocking appraisal. 'So, you have grown up like all little girls in the most delightful way. Your face is tear-stained, your little nose is shiny, but you will never look more beautiful.' He kissed the tip of her nose, her eyelids, the curly tendrils of hair at her temples, before finding her lips again. Presently he tilted her head with a gentle finger beneath her chin, and gazed down into her eyes.

'When will you marry me?'

'Marry you?' she answered, taken aback by all the terrifying delight which his words entailed. To marry him, to spend the rest of her life with him; to wear denim, yes, but beautifully cut, a tiny silk kerchief tied at the side of her neck to match the one at his firm brown throat. To be shamelessly in love with him for the rest of her happy life. For Joanna it could not happend too soon. 'When you wish,' demurely.

His eyes mocked her deepening colour. 'Afraid?' he whispered.

Joy so great that it hurt squeezed her heart. Joanna found herself taking his hand, holding it to her lips and speaking against the palm.

'I love you,' she said. 'I've almost despaired of you ever loving me.' She drew his hand along her soft cheek. 'Why did you buy Candida's portrait?'

'Because you had painted it. I wanted you and everything to do with you.'

He had to take her in his arms again then to convince her with kisses. He came to her like a consuming fire burning with his need of her, and Joanna knew he was hers. Her passion flared to meet his and he was the one who drew back, to say unsteadily, 'Now I can understand my Spanish ancestors insisting upon a duenna being present when their daughters received their intended. You, Juana *mia*, will certainly be in need of one if I stay much longer. Tomorrow we will buy your rings and your trousseau. Then we will fly back home and be married as swiftly as it can be arranged. Since I have waited so long for my marriage it is only right that my family and friends should share in our happiness. For myself it will be a great trial, waiting until we truly belong.'

He kissed her hair and drew her against him. Joanna sighed with pure bliss. Lovely to feel his heart beating against her, to face that ardent look in his eyes without lowering her own to hide her love for him. To wake up in the morning to find the sun warm on silk-panelled walls, on the bed where Ramón lay beside her, dark hair ruffled on his pillow, the delicious aroma of freshly made coffee which they would share on the edge of laughter.

Joanna hugged him in the sheer joy of living. Soon she would be deciding what she was going to wear for her wedding. She could not wait to be back again in the paradise from which she had been uprooted. Rosita would weep with joy, but Joanna was not so sure about Ramón's relations.

'Your grandmother, Ramón. What will she say to ... to our being married?' She lifted her face to gaze up at him with wide-eyed apprehension. 'You did say that she hated having her portrait painted.'

He laughed. 'Why, of course she hated having her portrait done at her age. There are so many of her when she was young and beautiful. However, she is very fond of it because she says you have given her a beauty of character in her face that she did not know she possessed.'

Joanna looked up at his lean face, loving it. 'Your *abuela* is still beautiful, so how could I portray her otherwise.'

'And, Juana *mia*, do you know why? Because she had a happy life, a wonderful marriage, and she was always kind. Like you. When she saw how it was with me she suggested having the portrait painted. She already loves you as her granddaughter. She is a romantic like you and believes in the fairies. But no matter. You are mine and no one is going to take you from me ever.'

'The arrogant Marqués,' Joanna said, loving him.

He lifted a mocking brow. 'I shall be even more arrogant when I have my lovely wife beside me. What do you say to that?'

Joanna looked solemnly up at him. She said humbly, 'I wouldn't have you any other way, and I wouldn't want to live without you.'

Joanna was having breakfast the following morning when her father walked in. He was wearing his dressing gown and sat down near to her bed. He was smiling.

'You know, Daddy, about Ramón and me? I can tell by your smile,' she said, on a feeling of anti-climax. The knowledge that she was, in a short time, to be Ramón's wife still took her breath away. 'Did you expect it?'

Tongue in cheek, Nick said, 'Let's say that I'm delighted.'

He rose from his chair, leaned over her breakfast tray and kissed her.

'Did Ramón tell you?' She watched him resume his seat.

Nick was still smiling. 'He came to the party last night to tell us. You know how reserved he is as a rule? Well, I've never seen him so happy. The party went on until the small hours. Later he and I strolled around London. We didn't go to bed.' He looked at his watch. 'That reminds me—he's coming for you at ten, something about rings and a trousseau.' He looked at her glowing face. 'You are happy. It wasn't Laurence, after all.'

She grimaced happily. 'You know it wasn't,' she teased, then added more soberly, 'How did the party go? What did Candida say about Ramón and me?'

Nick shrugged. 'She wasn't very coherent by the time Ramón arrived after taking you back to the hotel. I told Candida where he had gone and the next thing she was the life and soul of the party. I can only think that her success in the play and the praise of the critics I'd invited to the party went to her head. She was quite drunk by the time Ramón arrived, and after throwing her arms around his neck to congratulate him, she passed out. Laurence took her home later in a taxi. He said to tell you he's very happy for you and that if you need him at any time he'll always be there.'

Joanna's eyes were misty. 'Nice Laurence,' she murmured. 'Do you think Candida cared for Ramón?'

Again Nick shrugged philosophically. 'She might have done, but she's become a West End star overnight and isn't likely to throw that over her shoulder in favour of marriage even with a Spanish *marqués*. Now I think I'll go to bed.'

A few weeks later Ramón stood gazing with slight impatience at the crowd waiting to see him leave the island with his bride. Beneath a palm tree, Joanna, enchanting in her going-away outfit, was kissing her father, then a weeping Rosita, goodbye. In the weeks preceding the wedding Ramón had endeavoured to treat his beloved with the degree of impartiality demanded by Spanish society. But it had become difficult, almost impossible, loving her as he did. Everything had gone splendidly, the church service with Joanna looking like a flawless magnolia in her wedding dress, the reception, the speeches, and the quelling of his own need not to look at his enchanting wife too often for his own peace of mind. He was hopelessly in love with her and his need of her could hardly wait until such time as they would be alone. He tore his eyes away from his bride to flick an impatient wrist to consult his watch; any moment now they would be on their way; London, then Paris. He had bought a flat in each capital for them, and he smiled, picturing her delighted surprise when he presented her with the keys.

How lovely she was, with her honey brown hair sparkling in the sun no less than her eyes as she kissed everyone goodbye. Beneath his intent gaze it was not surprising that she should glance up at him to wrinkle her nose in the endearing gesture he had grown to love. Then, with an adoring look, she was running towards her very handsome, very impatient husband, and with a total lack of regard for propriety, flung herself into his arms to kiss him very thoroughly.

Needless to say, Ramón weathered remarkably well the

shock of a delicious bundle of femininity throwing her arms around his neck in public, and he did not cut the kiss short because of it. Joanna herself took longer to recover from the breath-stopping kiss and the hunger of his arms as she walked demurely with him into their plane.

Seated side by side, their hands met, their fingers dove-tailed together. As the plane screamed and shot forward to rise like a bird, their hearts as one rose with it. Quickly they kissed, snatching a little from the endless store of happiness awaiting them in their future life together.

May Paperbacks continued

THE MEDICI LOVER *by Anne Mather*
When Suzanne went to Italy for a short holiday with her friend Pietro, she hadn't foreseen that she would fall in love with his forbidding cousin Mazzaro di Falcone. And Mazzaro was an aristocrat, married, with a child – and divorce was out of the question. Was there any solution to Suzanne's problems?

BACHELOR TERRITORY *by Gloria Bevan*
Alison fled from one end of New Zealand to the other to avoid meeting a man who had turned her world upside down, a man she knew she would hate if she ever met him. Then, unbelievably, she *did* meet him – and found she wasn't hating him quite as much as she'd been expecting to. But how did *he* feel about her?

HARBOUR OF LOVE *by Anne Hampson*
Kirsty had made it quite clear to Flint Dawson that she didn't love him and never could; ironically, she herself was in love with a man who didn't return her feelings. So why did she find herself feeling put out when Flint took her at her word?

STRANGE ADVENTURE *by Sara Craven*
Young Lacey Vernon was being more or less forced to marry the Greek tycoon Troy Andreakis to save her father from ruin – but as time went on she began to realise, unwillingly, that perhaps she wasn't dreading him as much as she imagined she was. But that was before she learned what kind of a man Troy really was . . .

THE IMPOSSIBLE BOSS *by Jane Corrie*
Tammy Dainton hadn't come all the way out to the Australian outback just to be bullied and pushed around by that detestable, impossible man Rick Hatton – but Rick Hatton held all the cards, and it looked as if Tammy would just have to put up with him . . .

35p net each

Available May 1977